SAN

Henry Shukman's first book of fiction, ~~~~~
was published in 2004 to great acclaim. Having won
the Arvon International Poetry Competition in
2000, his first collection of poetry, *In Doctor No's
Garden*, won the Aldeburgh Poetry Festival Prize
and was shortlisted for the Forward Prize for Best
First Collection. He was selected as one of the 2004
Next Generation Poets.

ALSO BY HENRY SHUKMAN

Fiction

Darien Dogs

Poetry

In Doctor No's Garden

HENRY SHUKMAN

Sandstorm

VINTAGE BOOKS

London

Published by Vintage 2006

2 4 6 8 10 9 7 5 3 1

Copyright © Henry Shukman 2005

Henry Shukman has asserted his right under the Copyright,
Designs and Patents Act, 1988 to be identified as the author
of this work

This book is sold subject to the condition that it shall not
by way of trade or otherwise, be lent, resold, hired out, or
otherwise circulated without the publisher's prior consent in any
form of binding or cover other than that in which it is published
and without a similar condition including this condition being
imposed on the subsequent purchaser

First published in Great Britain in 2005 by
Jonathan Cape

Vintage
Random House, 20 Vauxhall Bridge Road,
London SW1V 2SA

Random House Australia (Pty) Limited
20 Alfred Street, Milsons Point, Sydney,
New South Wales 2061, Australia

Random House New Zealand Limited
18 Poland Road, Glenfield, Auckland 10, New Zealand

Random House (Pty) Limited
Isle of Houghton, Corner of Boundary Road & Carse O'Gowrie,
Houghton, 2198, South Africa

The Random House Group Limited Reg. No. 954009
www.randomhouse.co.uk/vintage

A CIP catalogue record for this book
is available from the British Library

ISBN 9780099468493 (from Jan 2007)
ISBN 0099468492

Papers used by Random House are natural,
recyclable products made from wood grown in
sustainable forests. The manufacturing processes
conform to the environmental regulations of the
country of origin

Printed and bound in Great Britain by
Bookmarque Ltd, Croydon, Surrey

CMD, again

La plus belle des choses, pour certains, c'est une troupe de cavaliers; pour d'autres, une armée de fantassins; pour d'autres encore, une escadre en mer. Et pour moi, c'est de voir quelqu'un aimer quelqu'un.

– Sappho (tr. Jacques Lacarrière)

ACKNOWLEDGEMENTS

Once again, many thanks to Dr Woof of the Wordsworth Trust for a decisive year as poet-in-residence at Grasmere, Cumbria; also to the Royal Literary Fund for a fellowship at Oxford Brookes University; and to Arts Council England for a writer's award of several years ago intended for this book.

Thanks also to the *Missouri Review* and *O. Henry Prize Stories*, in which some of this book first appeared. And to: Don Kurtz, Robert Boswell, Tom Paine, Rebecca Abrams, Rory Carnegie, Hamish Robinson, Peter Cowdrey, Alex Cohane; to Carol Ann, Sonny, Peter and Robin; and, most of all, to Clare.

1997

At six o'clock the bar on the east side of Seventh Avenue had just been found by the late sun. Mortimer watched as the smooth frosted panes of its four windows were suffused with a dense gold glow. They lit up like sheets of light: a hazy rich light as of a harvest sunset in the fields back home and long ago in the England of his childhood, which no longer existed; or as of the desert in the late afternoon when the torture of daytime was over, when at last the sun granted a reprieve and for half an hour, while it rested above the horizon, all things settled into themselves, bathed in light like a charm. Mortimer remembered how at that hour in the desert it was as if you had been asleep all day, your consciousness beaten into a dark corner, and now at last it woke up, came out of its cave and found the whole world waiting. He remembered how loose and fluid his limbs would feel, how happy he'd be to be standing on the dust in scuffed boots with nothing but the flat earth in all directions, every last foot of it empty of humanity, of vegetation, of clutter. It was a marvellous thing to be in the desert at the end of day. It was one of earth's prizes.

He thought of it now and was filled with emotion.

Tears threatened to come to his eye. Terrible, he told himself, you're a terrible, sentimental old soak.

He lifted his glass and drained it, then set it down beside a three-day-old London *Times* which lay folded into a cudgel on the bar top. He glanced at it, then twirled his finger at the barman. 'Another Ballantines.'

The barman nodded at the newspaper. 'Any news?'

'News?' Mortimer picked up the newspaper and shook his head.

But there was news, and he couldn't resist another look at it. They had taken to having snapshot obituaries in a column down the side of the main page these days. He had stumbled across it by chance, while browsing through the foreign pages, and he had been carrying it around with him ever since.

French photographer Celeste Dumas, 53, died last Wednesday at her home in Pau, south-western France, of bone cancer. Once celebrated for her adventurous work as a war photographer in the Sahara Desert, in collaboration with controversial British journalist Charles Mortimer, she was best known for her portraits of provincial and rural France, in particular of the Languedoc peasantry. Last year the Centre Pompidou held a retrospective of her work. She is survived by a husband and two daughters.

He might even have shown it to the barman – as if it might mean anything at all to him – but reading that epithet about himself again, decided he had better not.

Over here, not even the editor at the magazine where he sometimes worked seemed to have any idea how badly things had gone for him; or else they'd all forgotten. But back in London they hadn't, apparently.

He had a swig of his fresh drink and wondered: how befuddled, how silted up and muddy-headed had he let himself become that for so many years now he hadn't even thought of Celeste? He couldn't bear to, presumably. More than twenty years ago: he had been a young man, still starting out. And now, as an overweight, supernumerary hack who had lost his best contacts, been hounded out of London; now, when he was down and vulnerable, with a bad heart, with no dependable work, no aeroplane tickets in his back pocket waiting to ferry him to far-off disasters that had nothing to do with him personally – now that he was defenceless, there she was again, and it was far too late.

For a moment he couldn't move. There was that desert light before him, on the windows. Briefly he could see her face again, the colour of desert sand, her eyes streaked with shards of sunlight on rock. A hot breeze touched his cheek, and he could smell the wonderful dry aroma of dust, something like fresh plaster except it spoke of openness not of walls; of freedom not cramped and cramping houses – freedom from clouds, from cities, from people, from beasts, trees, from everything: freedom to go into the garden of God with a light heart.

1976

Mortimer gave copy the final word and hung up.

He pulled a Jazira cigarette from the paper pack on the table, drew the heavy glass ashtray closer and gazed out over the rooftops of Algiers. The impression was of a pale blue quilt, the square top of each house shining after a recent shower, reflecting the colour of the sky. It was a city of rooftops. In the distance he could see the sea looking like a sheet of zinc, calm under the departing rain clouds. The scene had the loveliness of any hot, dry country after it has been rinsed with rain.

It was good to be in a foreign city. He could have sat there gazing over the rooftops for hours. He had the sensation that he was surveying his own territory – own not in the sense of owning but belonging. This was his true home: a hotel room with a big ashtray, a solid desk and a splendid window overloooking an impoverished sprawl of humanity. And not just his home but his proper life, his modus vivendi. The city below was like a ploughed field busy germinating the fruits it would soon yield.

It was good, too, to be alone. For the first time he felt liberated from Saskia, his ex-fiancée, and sure it was right that they had separated. With a continent and a sea between them, he could cease worrying. He hadn't acted badly, it wasn't a failing on his part to have left rather than undertake a commitment that scared him more and more.

Mortimer felt he ought to be picking up the telephone and making a call but he had forgotten to whom, and why. Then it came back to him: room service, that was all. The week's work over, all copy filed, at least for the moment: time for a little reward, a glass of the sweet pink milk known as a *frappé*. He smiled inwardly when he remembered: nothing more onerous than that. It was good to have work under his own control: a cigarette, a note-book and a pink milkshake: all he needed.

The phone rang and he picked up the heavy black receiver, relic of an earlier decade.

'Nice. Very nice.' It was Kepple, the *Tribune*'s foreign editor, calling from London.

'How on earth do you know already?' Mortimer asked. He had finished giving his copy to London only minutes before.

'I read it as Mildred took it down,' Kepple replied.

'Well, don't start thinking such zeal gives you any special editorial rights,' Mortimer said.

'The "Great Wall of Africa",' Kepple chuckled. 'Excellent. That'll be the headline. You'll have to give us a few more on the region.'

'Of course,' Mortimer blurted without thinking.

Just the day before, Mortimer had returned to Algiers from the Western Sahara, where the Rio Camello guerrillas were fighting Morocco for a disputed territory. The war had been going on a year with barely a mention in the press. But recently the Moroccans had built a three-hundred-mile wall of sand across the desert in an attempt to keep out the guerrillas. It wasn't much more than a bulldozed dyke the height of a man, with military posts strung along it, but it was still a remarkable story.

Mortimer hadn't got as far as thinking where he might try to go next, but pleasure welled at the story's having gone down well. It was his first print story for some time. It would be excellent to stay in the region for now.

'I'll be taking it straight up to the boss,' Kepple went on. 'Bloody good stuff. The reportage too.'

Mortimer had scribbled a lot of notes about the guerrillas themselves while with them, and cobbled them together into a small feature.

Kepple started quoting back Mortimer's words: '"*They lounge by the fire like wild animals in repose, giving half their attention to their tea-making, keeping half on the alert. You've never seen people so relaxed. And in the middle of the Sahara, in the middle of a war. Tolstoy was right: there's no laziness like a military life.*"'

Kepple cleared his throat. 'Never fancied you for a travel writer. Nor for reading Tolstoy. We'll call that one "Tea on the Frontline", and run it alongside the main piece. I'll see if I can get the Sunday supplement interested in something too. We think you should go into the Atlas Mountains, then down south. I'll fill you in later.'

Even after five years in the trade – Mortimer would be celebrating his thirtieth birthday in a month's time – you couldn't be invited to contribute a series to the *Tribune* and not feel excited. Especially when this was his first story since his sojourn in television – a sojourn that now, already, he could see had been a hiatus in his real life. He'd always been a print man, always would be.

He'd been trying to get more foreign assignments for years. Mortimer had always longed to be a roving reporter. It was obvious to him: the thing to do with one's life was to travel. One had been given a number of decades in this sunny, tragic world – what else to do but explore and report back on what you saw? He couldn't imagine a greater freedom, and purpose with it. You had your notebook, your biro, your passport: you went where the wars were, and the earthquakes and famines.

His first few years in the papers had been nothing like that. He'd had the odd assignment abroad, and would come back bursting with a triumph of news-making, only to find the editor hadn't yet run it, and see it shunted day after day until it was out of date.

Most of the time was spent regurgitating information one had been given, and meanwhile dropping cigarette ends in half-drunk cups of coffee that had gone cold on the desk, or banging out paragraphs for other people's pieces where the editor wanted a change in angle, or driving through rain in small cars with overweight men from the paper who didn't bathe enough, eating Indian meals with them, sitting at pub tables crowded with glasses. All of which might represent a measure of his having arrived, or at least having got started – and also, he reflected occasionally, when in good spirits, that he was in the midst of an apprenticeship, was learning his trade on the job –

but it was a far cry from the global scope, the dusty suit, scuffed notebook and leaky local biro in a hot country, that he had once imagined.

Mortimer reflected how odd it was that he had had to move to television in order to be wanted, rather than tolerated, by a newspaper. There was no end to the respect television commanded. His year in it had been only a modest success, yet it had totally changed his status with the papers.

A month back he'd had a drink with Kepple, the *Tribune*'s foreign editor, in a bleak pub on the Gray's Inn Road.

'Why are we meeting here?' he'd asked.

'Scoping the new watering holes. In case we move.' The paper had been talking about moving from its Fleet Street premises for some time. 'So things didn't pan out on the small screen?' Kepple asked. 'Can't imagine why you'd want to leave it.'

'It wasn't my cup of tea.'

'I thought everyone wanted to be on the box.'

Mortimer shrugged. 'Not me.'

'Well, Bill told me to work something out' – Bill being the paper's proprietor. 'Says you were one of the good ones to watch. I've got just the ticket if you want it. Desert nomads turn guerrilla fighters. Starting up a righteous war all their own in the Sahara.'

'I'll need decent money,' he'd said.

'Bill is constitutionally disinclined towards new salaries this month, so he says,' Kepple had replied. 'He likes retainers better. Perfect for you. A decent retainer, and fees per story.'

'And expenses?'

'Expenses too, of course.'

Mortimer had gratefully taken on the job. It was just what he had been hoping for.

The Saharan assignment had also been just what he needed when it came to Saskia. With things being over with her, and his therefore being free to go, free as never before. And his needing to. Saskia had delivered a string of ultimatums on which he had failed to deliver, and at last she had meant it, and packed his bags for him. He had moved into the spare room of a friend, a lawyer with a young family. Mortimer's presence in that already fraught domesticity was too much: it had been an untenable situation. And on top of that, the English winter had been drawing on interminably. March already, and no sign of the sun since Christmas, hardly.

I'm like a mariner, Mortimer told his friends, I'm away too much. And when I'm not away I'm looking to go away. I never know when I'll be off next. It's no life for a partner. Saskia's done the right thing.

Or sometimes he said: *we*'ve done the right thing. Because it was mutual, more or less. True, it was he who had become ever more remote, ever less able to settle into home life, ever more fearful of the looming commitment, but it was she who had called their mutual bluff. And once they had started talking openly, it became clear they felt equally equivocal.

At least that was what they told themselves. He sometimes wondered if the real problem hadn't been different. He would think of their last formal talk about calling it all off. Formal was the word. They'd sat in her sitting room talking about the need to set one another free for something better. Mostly she had talked. He had listened, and in some way none of what they were saying had seemed true, or even important. He'd had the sense that they were putting up words like so much smoke, and the real story had nothing to do with what they said. They were wasting their breath. The truth, the real course of events, would come along regardless of their words. He'd felt an urgency to get away, as if only away from her, and away from their home, would he be able to order his thoughts and reconnect with the truth of the situation; and then be able to say the right things.

That had never happened. He had simply left.

And there had been the house too, his claustrophobia in it. It was her house, but within a few months of their meeting he had given up his shabby Bayswater studio, never much more than a place to lay his head, and transferred the rent to her mortgage. Sometimes he'd come in from the news desk at night and his first instinct would be to turn round and leave. It wasn't her; it was the house: to be boxed in a dark container of brick in the no man's land between the city centre and the suburbs, the transitional zone of endless terraces, some brick, some stucco, with the West End only twenty minutes away, but equally with a row of local shops at the end of the street, marking this as a district unto itself; and all the families clunking shut their doors each night on the world, sealing themselves in their own chambers: it was a frightening way to pass one's life. But then after half an hour with his feet propped on an afghan cushion, sprawled on the spread of kelims, with two or three glasses of wine inside him, he'd begin to feel, amid the ethnic clutter of the household – which was all her doing – a sense of calm again, of his life making sense, and of this home making a kind of sense. Sometimes he could almost have called the house a haven, a place of retreat. At least, he could understand how others might. He didn't think that he himself was a man who needed a retreat.

He told himself it was the perfect arrangement: he had taken a look at commitment, given it enough of a shot to know it wasn't for him, had cured himself of the dumb couple-hunger that afflicted so many of his generation, and would no longer hanker after the dull solace of domesticity.

Then along came a Saharan war on a plate, and an offer from a newspaper: there had been no decision.

2

Instead of calling room service, he decided to go down in person. He'd have his pink milkshake in the lobby lounge.

The Al Asra was Algiers' most distinguished hotel, a colonial legacy built like a municipal edifice of provincial France, which it more or less had been, with thick masonry, shutters on every window, and a mansard roof tall and steep enough to have two tiers of dormer windows, one of which was his.

The lounge, an area of low marquetry tables, stiff silk settees and ornate trellis-work, spread around the lobby, up and down changes in floor level. It all looked mock Arabic, rather than what it was, Arabic, and was all but deserted just now: a table of men drinking glasses of tea, and a blonde woman over in a far corner.

Mortimer stumbled as he took a step. The woman looked up from her book, and he recognised her as a French photographer who had been down in the desert the previous week, in the Rio Camello camps. He had hardly spoken to her then. There had been a pack of journalists covering a congress the guerrillas were holding, and he had seen her only once, and had noticed her because she was pretty.

When his glass of sweet milk arrived on its saucer he picked it up on impulse and walked towards her, threading through the tables and chairs of the dark interior, inspired to approach her by a feeling of bonhomie towards other journalists, kindled by his coup at the foreign desk. But as he made his way over, his mood changed to something nearer alarm. An acute shyness seized him. He couldn't now imagine spontaneously beginning an easy conversation with her, he would quickly have to prepare an opening line.

He wished he hadn't already got up and committed himself to speaking to her, or had waved or nodded first, done something to pave the way. Why was he nervous? He had nearly been married, he wasn't some teenage ingénue, he made adequate money, he'd held down decent jobs: there was no need for this unease. He had already

17

thought of a good first line, back when he had been sitting down and not worrying. He racked his brains for it now, and when he did miraculously find it, it no longer seemed a good line at all. But he was already upon her, he had to use it.

'Makes a change from the desert, doesn't it?' he said with an inward groan.

She looked up from the book in her lap, then down again, and snapped it shut. 'The desert?'

'We met, remember? With the Rio Camello.' He felt aggrieved: surely she couldn't have forgotten meeting him. True, they had done no more than shake hands, but there hadn't been that many foreigners down there. And he himself might be an unknown but his paper at least was famous. Another reason he'd noted her was that someone had told him she was working for *Le Monde*.

Perhaps she felt she needed to be discreet about having been there, Rio Camello being a sensitive issue locally. He felt himself blush.

'Well, do you want to sit down?' She smiled. 'What is your drink, by the way?'

He tried to make a joke: 'My drink? Scotch and soda.' There was an uneasy pause. 'That's my drink. What's yours?'

'At this time of day? Water.' She frowned at his glass of pink milk. 'You're telling me that's a Scotch?'

He laughed, out of nervousness. 'This is some strange milkshake. They dye it pink and load it up with sugar. I rather like it.' He nearly got back on firm ground then, but when she again invited him to sit down, and he did, there followed an impossibly awkward conversation. She seemed to miss everything he said, and yet at the same time to be two steps ahead of him. He imagined a pair of good dancers unfamiliar with one another might feel this way, able to see the sense in one another's moves yet unable to get in step.

Mortimer again wondered why he felt so nervous. She was beautiful, for one thing. He noticed it first in her eyebrows. They had a movement and shape that tripped one's heart up. She was blonde, more or less, but the eyebrows were a thatchy brown, curving up towards the middle, where they ended in serifs tucked towards the bridge of the nose. The nose was very good, strong and fine with a slight bump in the middle, as if once broken. Altogether she had an air of anything but preciousness, as if she didn't treat herself like the beautiful woman she was, but lived a rough-and-ready outdoor life. Which she probably did, being a photojournalist.

Or perhaps it was that she was a little older than he was, and had a successful life as a foreign news photographer. She'd be one of the lucky ones, with steady work that kept her overseas.

There was something familiar about her voice. When she spoke it was as if he could sense the deep part of her from which its timbre arose. It arrived loaded with intimacy. He couldn't explain it. When she laughed it was as if she gave herself up to laughter completely. At one point in that first conversation he was convinced he knew her well from somewhere, and a bewildering excitement ran through him.

They arranged to meet later and he went back to his room both delighted and scared, though he couldn't have said why. He flopped on the bed, exhaled as if out of relief, or from exhaustion, and discovered that really it was out of happiness. An Orthodox monk he had once met in Serbia had told him: the heart wants to soar up to God like a balloon. Why did he feel so good all of a sudden? He couldn't remember ever feeling so free, so light-hearted. He knew now what that monk had been talking about. He was full of a weightless joy. He saw a lake in mountains. He was living beside it, had all he needed just there. Beside the lake was a house, and in the house his one perfect companion. No need to go anywhere ever again. The lake had a name: joy.

Which wasn't her name. She was called Celeste: French, of course, but she had a dash of Spanish too in her blood, he later discovered. He couldn't remember meeting anyone with her forthrightness before. When they later found their birthdays were only days apart, give or take a few years, he was unsurprised.

It all seemed to happen by itself, as things did when one lived right: the Atlas to cover, then the Tuareg of the deep south; and a photographer planted by fate under his hotel roof.

That night at dinner in the medina he told Celeste his plans.

She listened, looking at him across the plastic-covered table. Her pale green eyes seemed to see into the pit of his belly, where her gaze touched a warm pool he hadn't known was there. Her irises were predominantly green, but streaked with gold, blood brown and sky blue. He fell silent. He could see her pupils flinch then swell slightly. They looked at each other longer than was necessary, long enough that he began to feel uncomfortable, to worry about how to end the stare, until he found he didn't want to.

Celeste had spent a month in the Maghreb already, she told him. She said that after the Far East, where she had been working for *Le Monde* and a Lyons paper for nine months, to be here felt like coming home. 'All the French names, the French buildings, and everyone speaks French. And Marseilles is just across the water,' she said with a smile that roused two sleeping dimples. 'I just finished a photo-essay for *Der Spiegel*, and I was thinking of going home. But I already feel I am.'

Later, in a crowded bus heading back to the hotel, Celeste whispered in his ear, 'You should take me with you.'

His heart bounced, and he found it hard to swallow.

In the morning, lying in his bed, he was filled with a strange numbness. He was waiting until it was nine o'clock in London. He was able to lie absolutely still. Already his limbs were anticipating being back in the desert. He loved the desert.

When it was almost nine he reached for the phone and called Kepple. 'I might want to bring a photographer along. You mentioned the Sunday magazine. Any chance of hooking up with them for some spreads?'

Did he have that kind of leverage? It was a mad idea.

It was premature, in every way, madly so, but she was right here, in the same hotel. And there was something about her. It wasn't just that he liked the way she looked; somehow he felt she might be part of the auspices blessing his return to print. And he felt a tingle of excitement in his bones, presage of a scoop, the kind that surprises even its subjects, coming so early they themselves hardly recognise the news they represent, yet which changes the landscape for a long time. He had to act on it at once. There would be untold advantages to having a photographer along, in fact now he could not imagine proceeding without one.

Kepple hesitated.

'Listen, if you're right about the Atlas Mountains,' Mortimer urged, 'if Monsieur Taillot is right —' Taillot was a contact the paper had given him whom in fact he had yet to call — 'then this will be big and we'll need pictures. It'll be too late to send someone later.'

Where this new boldness came from he didn't know.

Kepple grunted. 'Well, there's not just the Atlas. You should go south too, down into the desert. There's the drought in Mali, for a start. And the Tuareg. Bill seems keen on you. He just dropped me another note saying he wants more. He even cracked a joke, called you Mortimer of the Maghreb.'

Kepple let out a groan of reluctant assent. 'Leave it to me.'

3

From the café window, across the square, Mortimer could see a ship leaving port. Its stern seemed to swivel across the water without the vessel making any headway. To the side of it a faint brown stain hung against the milky sky. Meanwhile, in the street, all the *petits taxis* and *grands taxis* put up their aroma of exhaust, with here and there a grey plume hanging above the traffic. And in the café, on the square, on the street corners, wherever you looked all the men were smoking. This was a city whose life, if you wanted in any way to join it, you did first by smoking.

Mortimer sat smoking himself in the big café on the Place Al-Ghazi, a bare, canteen-style establishment full of plastic chairs and faux-marble tables. There were no women in it at all, just a throng of black-haired men. They served coffee and mint tea in small or large glasses, and local sodas coloured bright orange and lawn green.

When Monsieur Taillot arrived, both of them immediately lit up. They would chain-smoke for the half-hour they were there.

Taillot was indeterminately Mediterranean. Even his accent was hard to place: American-educated, perhaps, over a gravelly base that Mortimer thought might have been Corsican.

The conversation started to grow serious.

'Look,' Taillot said, sipping from his little, gold-enamelled glass of tea, 'this is dangerous stuff, believe me. If you don't watch yourself you'll get in trouble. The Atlas, they used to be like the Alps. Not any more. It's turning into the Wild West. Nobody knows what to do, except to keep beefing up the arsenal. Everybody's doing it, Brits, Americans, French, and the Russians too, the arms contracts keep coming in. The last thing anybody wants is another civil war here in the heart of the Maghreb.'

Taillot was an international observer, but in whose pay Mortimer had no idea.

'But who is the enemy?' Mortimer asked.

'That's Algeria's problem. They don't exactly know. But presumably it's village chieftains and such. The mountain villages have leaders who are also imams, or mullahs, religious men. But the Algerians have a history of invisible soldiering, as we all know.'

Taillot was clearly alluding to Algeria's struggle for independence.

'The real problem for the West is that the current president has been a pleasant chap, helping out with Iran and Iraq and so on, always ready to talk. His neutrality is extremely useful. He has leverage not only with Arab states but the Eastern bloc. The West would hate to lose him.' He cleared his throat. 'But there's more.'

Taillot drew out a Marlboro and twirled it in his fingers. Mortimer held out his lighter, and sensed by a slight hesitation that Taillot didn't want the cigarette lit so soon. He had planned to toy with it a little longer. Probably he wanted to tease Mortimer too, force him to draw out the clincher, beg for it: what more was there, please tell.

Mortimer looked around for a waiter and leaned back

in his chair. 'More tea?' he asked Taillot when the boy arrived.

A moment later, each with a lit cigarette in hand and a refilled glass of tea, Taillot said: 'Yes, there's much more. The Blue Menace.' He squinted at Mortimer as he drew on his cigarette.

Mortimer racked his brains. This was either a clue or something he ought to know. Whoever this Taillot was, Mortimer had been getting the impression increasingly that he was a significant player, requiring deference. Mortimer needed to show he was worthy of his confidences. He succeeded in disguising the inward 'Ah' he felt when he understood. 'You're talking about the Tuareg, *les hommes bleus*. They're a problem?'

Taillot nodded.

'But they simply roam the desert, they go where they please.'

'And where they please now is their own state. They have declared a nationhood, written a constitution. In Tamashek. Their language, as you know.'

Mortimer didn't know. He nodded. There was a pause.

'What does Kepple know of all this?' Mortimer asked.

Taillot squinted at him again, then shrugged.

Mortimer left it. It wasn't important. It crossed his mind that Taillot might even not know who Kepple was; or who Mortimer was for that matter: it was a dizzying thought, however implausible.

'The government is anxious to keep a lid on things. That is why you would be even more careful, if you decided to go to the deep south. The place you start is

Tamanrasset. Over the mountains, down in the middle of the desert. That's where the Tuareg are moving in. Coming down from the Hoggar Hills and the Southern Erg, we hear.'

'The Southern Erg?' he asked.

'The sand sea, the ocean of dunes. A natural home to the Tuareg only.' He smiled. 'A formidable place.'

Taillot had a stippling of pockmarks on his left cheek: only the one cheek, Mortimer noticed. 'Is all this new?' Mortimer asked.

'There have been rumblings. Even in the last century, under the French, some Tuareg wrote a declaration of independence. But it never meant anything. It's a huge area of sand, unpoliceable. To be perfectly frank, Algeria would have half a mind to let them have what they want, if the government had not been investing so heavily in the Sahara. The desert is the president's golden dream, a huge untapped resource. Algeria's Amazon, he calls it.'

'A resource for the construction sites of the world?'

Taillot tutted. 'There's much more than sand. Minerals of all kinds. And water too; it just happens to be a hundred metres below ground. And other things. But a Tuareg state with a bite of Mali, a chunk of Niger, Mauritania and a whole lot of Algeria would be more than viable. And how do you stop them? They are completely nomadic. If their intentions get to be widely known, it could have an effect in the mountains, with the imams of the Atlas, who might start thinking: this unholy state of Algeria is crumbling, Allah's time has come.'

Taillot took a long draw on his cigarette. Mortimer

was enjoying himself, and had an equally deep puff on his own. 'Not only that,' Taillot continued, 'but Westerners *like* the Tuareg. If Algeria declares war on them, not only will it most likely fail to defeat them, the enemy being consummately elusive, it would bring a lot of ill feeling. The West has a romantic attachment to the nomads. They're one of Algeria's assets.'

Who was this man? Mortimer wondered. And why was he happy to brief him?

'So far, of course, nothing has actually happened. Or so one is led to believe. But I've heard rumours of Tuareg skirmishes in the deep south.'

'With who?'

'The police, of course. The gendarmerie. Technically, you could call it civil war.'

4

Mortimer would never forget his very first television story: the window panes of a Kirghiz hotel room had burst in, the glass showering over the bed and floor. Outside two tanks growled in the street below. Mortimer and the producer had hurled themselves to the floor. Mortimer had looked up at the broken windows, and seen a hole knocked through to a bigger world. The glass pouring in like water had seemed his baptism in the currents of his day. And Harry, the producer, with his flayed-looking face of ghastly redness, his flaming scalp, the remains of his grey hair permanently straggling upwards like wisps of smoke, had called him a genius for bringing them here. And the MiG that had come hurtling over the little city as he did his first ever piece-to-camera up on the hotel roof, his next stroke of luck: with its sharp beak and short ungainly wings the fighter plane had pulled a turn, then tipped up and shot into the sky as if running up glass rails. As it climbed, a bright point of phosphorescence went chasing up after it, wobbling slightly as it raced through the sky, gaining on the plane. Then it vanished. For a moment nothing happened. Then white streaks fanned across the sky and where the plane had been, a black ball of smoke hung absolutely still. The streaks shot out and down like fireworks, leaving trails that gradually dissolved into the blue.

Jimmy the cameraman had got it all, and it made the lead story on the bulletins two days later, the films having been rushed out in the diplomatic bag on the evening flight to Paris.

'Not a bad start,' said Harry. And just for those first few days, Mortimer had felt what it meant to live right, to live at the speed life intended for you.

It was only with the second story, about a supposedly bombed-out village that might in fact have collapsed in an earthquake – a possibility they didn't mention – that the compromise, the theatre, the constricting brevity of television began to irk him. So too its unwieldiness, requiring a whole team, and the shameless theatrics of it: the very purpose of the camera was often laughable: you were just looking at faces you might just as well have been listening to on the radio. When there was anything worth filming, half the time it was staged.

Over the months, he'd felt more and more constrained by television, as if the medium wouldn't let him do what he was good at, whatever that was.

But now, here in Algiers, once again he could feel the thrill of that first moment in the hotel room in Kirghizia: once again he was living right, and the right things would happen. Except that now it was even better: he was answerable only to himself.

They jumped on a train the next morning. It was Celeste's idea. They needed to get moving right away, she said. They could neither afford nor bear to wait for the Wednesday flight into the mountains. It was reckless to travel overland, and Mortimer couldn't exactly have explained how it came about, but effectively he found himself hitch-hiking across the Sahara over the coming weeks, with a beautiful French photographer at his side. Instead of reaching Tamanrasset in a couple of hops, and in one day, it would take them weeks. Or it would have done had they ever reached it.

In the morning, on the train, in the soft, dusty sunshine, Mortimer was filled with an inordinate sense of well-being. The guards had not closed the doors, and while Celeste sat at one of the tables, Mortimer stood on the steps clutching the bars and watching the suburbs pass by. There was such a pleasure to being one's own boss. The paper had put their trust in him. Whatever happened, whatever stories he came up with, it was all up to him.

It wasn't that the warm breeze on his face with its smell of diesel smoke exhilarated him, so much as filled his legs with a tingling warmth.

A strip of wasteland ran along the tracks. Beyond was a dirty white wall with scrap metal heaped on the far side. Then they crossed a little river, its banks strewn with rubbish. A boy sat on a rock beside four sheep that picked at the dirt. These ragged sights on the edge of the city seemed quiet, harmonious – as if away from the city's bustling heart peacefulness reigned over these scrappy, uncared-for things.

A hillside ahead was covered in a mosaic of little houses, some red, some pinkish, some white, and altogether resembled an intricately woven, pleasingly faded carpet.

He had an urge to grab Celeste and point these things out to her. It was good to know she was sitting just a few yards away, also travelling in the rattling iron beast that would take them far across this land, into the mountains and beyond, to the sand.

The train rode up the coastal plain into the foothills of the Atlas. It was a spring day, the hills sparkling, draped with gauzes of mist. Mortimer hardly knew what he was on his way to. They passed through rolling country where here and there men with pairs of small oxen ploughed little fields, long switches in hand. On some plots they had no oxen and three or four men would be stooped over hoes, ploughing by hand. Mortimer reflected what back-breaking work that must be, and what a household disaster a bad back could be. It was pleasant to witness all the small-scale husbandry.

Then the train slowed, the bends became longer and more frequent, the bridges and tunnels too, as they began to climb into the mountains.

Once, while he was standing to get a book from his bag on the overhead rack, as the train clackety-clacked over a girder bridge across a small ravine, nudging from side to side as it went, the carriage jolted and he swung against Celeste. She was warm and he didn't seem so much to fall against her as pour into her. It was a strange sensation. He pulled himself up and apologised but his heart was in his mouth. He glanced at her, and she was looking at him, her eyes bright, her lips open. In a flash he saw himself bending down and kissing her there and then.

But he didn't. He laughed lightly in response to her look, and said, '*Excusez-moi*,' as he sat down again.

The track flanked the side of a mountain now, and out the window a great view opened up through fir trees of the coastal plain already far below. What had seized him? How come everything had happened so fast? Here he was on a train heading towards a series of stories for the *Tribune* with a woman who already caused him sensations he had not known before. He could feel fate pressing in, trammelling and accelerating his life.

They got talking to a young man in black-rimmed glasses, a schoolteacher returning home from Algiers to spend the holidays with his family, who lived in the mountain town of Setif. They were getting off there too, and he insisted they come for lunch at his parents' house.

'But your mother,' Celeste said, 'what will she say?'

'She'll be happy. *Très heureuse.*'

Celeste raised her eyebrows at Mortimer as they stood just outside the antique station building, beneath its fringe of elaborate wrought ironwork, and he could think of no reason not to accept. They'd need lunch anyway.

The young man embraced a girl of eleven or twelve wearing a white housecoat over a pair of trousers, and a white scarf on her head, and introduced her as his sister, who had come to meet him, then led them off through the quiet, broad streets of the little mountain city. As he had promised, the family home was not more than ten minutes away.

The mother, a small round woman in a blue dress and white scarf like her daughter, her face a shiny pale brown, embraced all of them warmly, even the newcomers, and even her daughter who had probably not been gone more than twenty minutes, so overcome was she at her son's return. She bundled some notes into the daughter's hand and sent her off with a few words of soft Arabic.

The young man smiled. 'Very nice lunch. Just wait a little while. Come. Sit.'

He led them into a garden at the back, where they sat on home-made wooden benches. Small lemon and orange trees grew out of rusty tins. A border along the house was bushy with mint. Further down, a washing line criss-crossed the yard, hung with recently washed clothes that had dripped dark lines on to the cement beneath them. Fat drops bulged from the hems of the skirts and shirts, awaiting their turn to fall.

Mortimer saw all these things and was inordinately

delighted. This seemed somehow the perfect house for a family, the ideal yard where its various chores and functions could be carried out.

The mother came out with a tray of glasses and a jug of freshly made lemonade. The glasses were wet, just rinsed, and the drink was tepid but delicious. She apologised for having no ice, but the electricity had been down two days. They all heard the front door, and the mother went back inside.

An hour later they settled round the table to a large casserole of tripe stew. At the smell of it, Mortimer, a life-long disliker of offal, felt his heart sink in exactly the way it had when he had been a schoolboy, and lunch in its aluminium serving dish turned out to be liver or kidney. He glanced at Celeste, who happened to catch his eye across the table. She frowned at him, muttered, '*Ça va?*' then shaking her head mouthed, '*Pas?*'

He sent her a quick look of dismay. She smiled.

'*Madame,*' she began, '*Excusez-nous. Moi, j'aime bien*, but he is not accustomed to eating *les tripes*. They don't do it in England. *Nous nous excusons.*'

The woman needed no more prompting. She apologised profusely, Mortimer did the same, and she instructed the son to serve everybody else while she went back to the kitchen to make Mortimer an omelette, in spite of his protestations.

Mortimer was embarrassed but Celeste seemed to find the little incident endearing, and after lunch as they walked into town to a *place* where they could hire a taxi, she linked her arm in his and leaned against him. His heart jumped, and he spontaneously put his other hand on her forearm and squeezed her wrist, feeling her slender bone through its sleeve of muscle.

'Thank you,' he said, and she turned to smile at him. He almost lost his footing, seeing her face from so close, feeling the warmth of her skin, the heat of her breath. He could not help himself, and the next thing he knew he was standing in the sunshine of the street, hearing the quiet sounds of a city all but free of traffic, holding her face in his hands like a chalice, and kissing her. He could feel her cheeks smiling as she kissed him back, then they went slack, then slightly concave.

The kiss surprised both of them, awkward, clumsy, hungry, and not long. She pulled back, caught her breath, wiped her mouth and said, 'Not here.' And gave him another peck on the lips and hugged him. 'We must wait.' She leaned her forehead against his. 'Even if it's hard.'

It was hard. Mortimer was left yearning for more, but also with a keen sense of the impropriety of kissing in public, a sense of shame even, which both shadowed and amplified the dizziness of his hunger to kiss her again. In the end it was six days before they could be alone together. Mortimer felt he had never waited so long for anything.

5

They hired a Toyota to take them to Batna, where the paper had given Mortimer a contact, and they could get to work. The prospect of work offered a welcome shelter from the intense awkwardness he was experiencing. He couldn't account for it: she was hardly the first woman he'd been with. Yet it felt as if she was.

They were quickly drawn into a company of Berber farmers and part-time mystics, quiet men with Sufi leanings, with whom Mortimer fell into profound conversations about the nature of life while strolling through apricot orchards. One, a farmer called Ahmed, took him up into the hills above his farm, on a long walk through a eucalyptus forest to a waterfall. All Ahmed wanted, he said, was to live as God intended. He described Mortimer's journalism as the footprints he left behind him as he walked through life. It seemed a pleasing idea.

In the evenings they sat about the earthen floors of huts, among circles of men chewing dates and sucking sheep's milk from a shared cup. They allowed Celeste to join in because she was not only a journalist too, but also his wife (there could be no question about that).

'The best way to eat dates, the best way to drink milk,' Ahmed said of the date-and-milk combination. It was delicious, and made a good evening's indulgence. Alcohol didn't cross Mortimer's mind. He began to feel a bit holy himself, in such simple and trusting company. He even found himself wishing he really was married to Celeste, and did not have to lie about it. Yet he was glad too, somehow, that they had yet to consummate things. He felt like a child again, as if they were both children, side by side. In some still vaguer way he began to feel that they already were effectively married. He had never known one before, but in spite of spending so little time with her, he already felt he understood for the first time what a soulmate was. Deep down, a similarity of composition bound them, as if they were made of the same substance – which wasn't a figure of speech but an experience. When he was with her, he became aware of a bedrock within, and felt how it matched the equivalent in her: two tectonic plates meeting. It made him inexplicably at peace. When apart, he carried with him a sensation of this substratum: it had been brought to his attention by virtue of having met its twin. He would have talked about it with her had he been able to find a way. Sometimes he felt there was nothing to say on the subject that she didn't already know.

One late afternoon they found themselves alone on the packed dirt of the farm compound. They strolled out under olive trees and sat on a low mud wall. Before them the valleyside fell away in silvery-green foliage, and the far side shone like a sleek horse's flank.

'How's the story?' she asked.

Her face was flushed, her eyes sparkled and her pale lips parted, revealing the white tips of her teeth. There was something about her face, so open and full of intention. It made him dizzy.

He swallowed. 'I should get two, I think.'

She raised her eyebrows almost apologetically. 'Good idea to come.'

'Don't thank me,' he anticipated. 'It's good for me to have you.'

He looked ahead but could feel her presence at his

side so strongly, such a warmth beside him, that he hardly saw what his eyes were looking at.

The local imam was becoming a cause célèbre. Wild-looking men with rifles slung over their shoulders arrived in the town and danced in circles, shooting their guns into the sky. Celeste photographed them. Mortimer wasn't sure how they'd take to the sight of a camera, but it had an invigorating effect on them, he could feel it. The celebrations became more intense, louder, with more firing off of the guns. It was almost as if the festivities had now discovered their real point, once the lens was on the scene. Then the men all went off to pray with the imam.

He sat on his dais for hours on end, preaching and chanting. Mortimer tried to get an interview with him but could find no one willing to interpret. Celeste photographed a whole field of men bowing in prayer, with the little old man far away, alone on his makeshift stage.

The paper took the image, and another of the riflemen dancing and letting off their guns, a cloud of gunsmoke drifting over their heads. They ran a story: *Islamist militants finding a focus in the Atlas Mountains.* Two weeks later the imam was killed, an event which triggered a sequence of reprisals against the state authorities, and threatened to bring down a general disaster on the province, though in fact that wouldn't arrive for a few years yet.

Mortimer slept on the floor of one hut, Celeste on a cot in another, along with three women and several children.

When they finally came down out of the mountains in the back of a Peugeot estate car, winding past springs tucked into the nook of hairpin bends, through olive and orange groves, down hillsides of vine and across meadows of tough, scrawny-looking flowers, they had hardly had a minute alone together since the train ride six days earlier. Sitting in the car, he felt so close to her she burned against his side. He knew, he was sure, that she wanted to be alone with him as much as he did with her.

They came round a bend of rock to see below them, where there ought to have been land, a broad, gold cloud stretching away like a sea. Only once they descended into the cloud did dark lines begin to show, marking where irrigation dykes ran across a plain, then faintly the outlines of shrubs appeared, and rows of young crops, and finally the red earth itself. By then they were on the outskirts of Touggourt.

Touggourt was a small city, and clung to the foot of the Anti-Atlas. It had a heart of palms, red mosques and labyrinthine alleys. The streets were aromatic with stores selling grilled chicken and couscous. At night they filled with the smoke of vendors grilling brochettes over charcoal, with the dust the crowds kicked up from the dirt streets, and all the palms and eucalyptus – the hardy trees that survived on little water – were coated in dust too, and seemed to hover amid the clouds of drifting smoke. It was as if the purpose of a settlement were nothing other than for humanity to put up all this smoke and bustle and noise, its one big smoke signal.

They checked into the best hotel. It was their first night

alone together, in a double bed, in a room whose door they could lock, with their own bathroom. Mortimer found he had developed a sense of sanctity towards his own body, and towards Celeste. As soon as the bellhop, a man in a dusty brown jellaba, closed the door, another cataclysmic shyness seized him, the worst yet. The room seemed quiet, too small. Just a few faint Arab-city sounds reached them through the blinds: someone calling, mopeds going by, someone hammering on metal a few streets away. He went to unzip his bag, and the sound of the zip seemed to fill the room, and also to cry out: this is the action of a nervous man. He hadn't realised how much shelter those holy men in the mountains had been offering. Suddenly there was no escape, no refuge. For a moment, crouching at his bag, he felt that he would not be able to rise to his feet, so enormous was the feeling running through him: a nameless feeling, one that made it impossible to pluck up one single word, let alone string two together. Then he did stand up and immediately thought he would have to drop into a crouch again. He turned and saw she had gone, then realised he could hear the fan humming in the bathroom. A moment's relief. He lay on the bed. But there was no relief. They were the worst ten minutes he could remember. He was trapped in a plain room in a desert town in the presence of something that had the power to swallow him whole.

Everything felt preordained: her half-drunk bottle of Sidi Ali water on the black bedside table. His having filed a third story on the mountains, being on his way to something bigger. His unzipped but still packed bag. The clothes he was wearing – jeans, faded blue shirt with salt lines faintly showing, stiff with dust, boots whitened by road dust. His six days' stubble, his hair thick with dust. The quiet thunder of the shower running in the bathroom. And his own rapturous terror. He had surely experienced all these things before, or had known all along that he would one day. He was transfixed. He ought to take a shower too but he couldn't move. Behind the bathroom door the water roared quietly. The sense of the moment's inevitability pressed in on his ears. For a moment his vision seemed bleached by desert dust, desert sun, and by this dust storm of emotion. Fate, he thought, was a lion that tore a life to pieces. It picked you up in its jaws and shook you. Whatever you thought, you were helpless really. You could do nothing but submit to what happened to you. That Saskia had finally and irrevocably left him at Christmas, that he no longer had to worry about that particular compromise, that he was staying on in the Maghreb, in the desert, had come down here in the first place – all these things were subsumed by inevitability, by a fate in which part of him too conspired. The current that carried him also had its unseen source in him.

Just before she opened the door he had time to reflect that perhaps the experience he was undergoing had nothing to do with her. The idea brought relief. But the moment she emerged wrapped in a towel all the dread welled up again, and he knew it had everything to do with her. She went straight to her case on the floor by the window. She squatted down, legs held together by the towel, and lifted the lid. Then she stood and pulled the faded red curtain across the window. She rummaged in her case, found something and blew her nose twice lightly. Then she stood and came to the bed.

He was sure she came intending to give him a hug. Perhaps they'd have a snooze in one another's arms. But as soon as he felt the bed give under the weight of her knee he knew what would happen. It could hardly have been a surprise, he reflected later, yet it felt like one. She said, '*Enfin*', and loosened her towel. He opened his arms and burrowed, eyes closed, towards her face. He felt the curtain of damp hair against his temple, her breath hot on his shoulder, and she gave a little hum, then made a movement after which the towel had come away. Her skin was warm, damp. They were immediately into a deep kiss. When he interrupted things to untie his bootlaces he felt faint.

She was acrobatic, her stomach had internal engines of its own, a miniature sluice-station he learned to manipulate so it pumped against his fingers. The deeper she let him conduct her into her own pleasure, the further he went into his own. She held her ankles and soaked his face. He had never known anything like it.

'This sex is actually interesting,' he said later. He meant: it's not just something we do because we know we should, which had essentially been Saskia's position; his position too with most of his one-offs: it was necessary, surely, to satisfy one's desire. But this was a different matter: here was a new land asking to be explored.

'Just for the record,' he said, 'just in case there's any

doubt, I have strong feelings.' He couldn't remember ever feeling so unequivocal.

Her body was evidently not that young. There were even faint lines, ghosts of lines, on her breasts. But he loved their shape and weight; and her prominent nipples, almost without aureolas, seemed to state something about who she was. Her body was her instrument and she used it. They spent two days in the room, breaking off now and then to eat kebabs in the hotel restaurant, priming themselves for more. They ordered wine but hardly touched it. Once he guzzled a bottle of beer straight down. Gauzy twilights, dusty dawns came and went. Going to sleep was like walking along the edge of a cliff. He felt queasy, excited, fearful all at once. And woke to find the same feeling still there.

When eventually they ventured into the town its raucous din was delightful.

6

Touggourt

Essence, the man puts on my boots. Petrol. That's ingenuity for you. Petrol, and a sharp little knife with which, after scraping it back and forth on the pavement by way of sharpening, he actually manages to restore my boots to a semblance of their original suede.

A pleasant scene. Morning sunshine. A range of hills just visible in the distance, not yet eaten up by haze. And here under the umbrellas set in wheel hubs a number of men industriously scrubbing one another's shoes, and a far greater number sitting about watching. Shadows flit across the sunlit paving as the bustle of the morning goes by. I give him twice the accepted Nizara price. I too am a Nizara, apparently, a Nazarene, a white.

But I am avoiding the issue. To wit, la fille, la jolie blonde. Jolie yes, blonde yes, but hardly a fille. I'd say thirty, on balance. A touch older than I. But then she is travel-cured: could be as young as twenty-seven. Though there's a worldliness to her that betokens the crossing of life's watershed (i.e. three-o). Strange, considering the last three days, that I don't know her age. Will make enquiries.

Why do I feel so chirpy? What a question! Three days of bedroom acrobatics, mon brave! (I was about to say: because I'm away from rainy England and all its (my) problems. And truly if someone asked me now: you're never going to see the white cliffs again, how do you feel?, my answer would be: relieved, there's a few issues I no longer need worry about.)

She is something else. This is something else. Not sure I want to defile it, or her, with ink.

Dust and smoke and noise and bustle. Smells of exhaust fumes, of swept-up dust, of cooking, wine, rotting fruit — these are what cities properly consist of, this is what the South does properly, in a way the North cannot match. Out in the road a boy twirls a length of thread round and round his head, making twine, right in the midst of gurgling mopeds streaming past. Meanwhile, a donkey cart is negotiating him and his string, and a minibus is overtaking the cart, as well as all the mopeds. The principle of traffic here is not to stop. If no one ever stops then all can predict oncoming trajectories and pre-empt likely collisions.

What an effect the simple press of humanity has in a desert town. The buses and little Peugeots, and people everywhere, so many of them: a marvellous thing, at once exciting and reassuring. They create a sensation unknown in the West. The dust of multitudes drifting up as a haze into the unencumbered sky. The knowledge of the desert, the emptiness, all around. The desert forces a graphic understanding of the true human presence on the planet: a something, in a void.

Celeste's Frenchness: he was in love with it. He loved the way she had emerged from the bathroom that first time. '*Voilà, ça y est, enfin,*' and she slipped the towel's knot and let it fall, and for the first time he saw those small breasts, firm nipples. The buds themselves were large, the size of the little incense cones people burned in braziers throughout the country. During lovemaking they became perpendicular. They were one simple thing he appreciated about her. He tried to draw up a kind of chart to get some perspective, but a nagging anxiety that she might discover it held him back. He wanted to title it 'Pro and Con', assuming that there would be cons. Then changed it to 'Things I Like'. Then crossed out 'Like' and wrote 'Love' in smaller cursive.

It was hard to know how to categorise. Sexual and non-sexual? But where did each begin and end? Her hair, for example. There was no question he found it sexy. It was partly the colour, an ash blonde with brown, grey and rust all in there too, along with the shining sun-cured blondeness. It was a good length, long enough to do things with, like pull into a ponytail, or have hang down either cheek, but also short enough to leave serviceably all to itself. It seemed to him the perfect hair. Which was precisely why he had to sit down and write about it, along with everything else about her, to try and stick at least the tip of his nib of rationality into the crack, which must surely still exist, between himself and his feelings; between him and her.

She had a basically though not perfectly flat stomach, and Mortimer had noticed sometimes when she walked a hint of flare at the top of her thighs. He wasn't a connoisseur of women, yet there was something about her Frenchness that encouraged him to be. It was hard to define, but she put time and thought into her appearance: she had an agreeable workaday vanity, and it would have been a negligence on his part not to appreciate it.

She was a working woman who kept her eye on her job, yet at the same time was feminine, able to think about her attractiveness to men. Part and parcel of this was her body: lithe, supple, strong, and incidentally lovely. She was even capable of doing herself up for lovemaking – showering, shaving here and there, pulling on decorative underwear – in the same workmanlike spirit, which did not make it any the less sexy. If anything more so. But then she was anything but workmanlike once they got down to it. He discovered a few nights in that there had been a little lesbianism in her past, and he attributed her openness to that. She didn't hesitate to request, explain, insist. She was quite unlike the repressed Englishwomen he had known, whose lovemaking was blind and sudden. And she was good about getting to know his specifics too. All in all, in bed it was good in a way that was not lavish and extravagant, likely to be soon exhausted, but honest and candid. Mortimer had never enjoyed a relationship so much, even in the earliest days.

Gratitude at her having elected to come with him welled up again and again.

'I love doing this with you,' he said. 'Of course I always like it but this is different. I could go on and on. It almost doesn't feel like sex.'

'What does it feel like?' She was lying very still on the pillow, eyes glazed, in a moment of calm when her whole body's peace seemed to exude through her irises.

For just a second he thought of an answer among words such as: exploration, investigation, discovery.

He kissed her soft lips that were resting and restoring, and couldn't bring himself to pull his mouth away. Without breaking the kiss, he said, 'You know what it feels like.'

Above and around him the room filled with thick darkness. They lay still, mouth to mouth, forehead to forehead.

At other moments – tidying up their blankets, straightening the sheets while she was in the shower – he felt sick, as if truly ill and suffering. His midriff almost hurt, so sharp was the talon sunk in it. At any time – as he brushed out a hair from their undersheet, as he poured her a glass of mineral water from the bottle beside the bed – that claw could give a tug, or even just a tweak, and release a spasm of yearning.

He and Celeste talked a lot those first days, yet when he looked back on it later, it was as if all their lovers' talk had just been background music, the soundtrack to unfolding love, and they had hardly talked at all. So many intimacies exchanged, yet they were strangely forgettable, as if every precious word of self-revelation was just a crayon stroke in a brass rubbing, its purpose being to reveal a truer image beneath the words; which in some sense he already knew. Those days passed in a dream, or as if he were on drugs, caught in a process over which he had no control, and to that extent were perhaps nowhere near as self-revelatory as they seemed. Yet in the few short weeks they had together, he gained a sense of who she was, and of who he himself was, that he carried with him the rest of his life.

7

There was a knock on the door. A voice called, '*Venez, monsieur, venez. Téléphone.*' Mortimer stepped into his shoes.

A telephone receiver lay on the reception counter in the lobby. '*Oui?*'

It was Taillot. Kepple must have told him where Mortimer was.

'You can't go south,' Taillot said. 'It's out of the question.'

Mortimer waited for more. None came. So he asked: '*Pourquoi?*'

'It would be suicide.'

He waited again. 'Is that a threat? I assume it isn't.'

'Don't be a fool. Of course not. It's out of control down there.'

What did he mean by 'it'? He clearly hoped Mortimer would accept it as 'the situation'. Why then had Mortimer seen an expedition of backpacking students cheerfully trundling off in their Unimog the previous day, on their way to the Hoggar Hills near Tamanrasset, in the deep south? Why had two German trainee doctors gurgled out of the hotel yard that very morning in their VW van, heading south? Was Taillot trying to scare him off the story? If so, why? Somehow he felt it might be a good sign.

An ambiguous answer was the answer. He said: 'I'm always careful. Thank you.'

'There's also the sandstorms,' Taillot went on. 'It's the season for them, you know, the worst time to be in the desert.'

'Of course,' he muttered. 'Thanks again.'

Taillot's information-giving back in Algiers must have been far from disingenuous. Whoever had been telling Taillot what to feed the press had perhaps changed their mind. But who was it?

He told Celeste about the sandstorm part of the conversation, and was about to mention the rest of it, but something made him hold back.

The town had a hammam. 'You've never been?' Celeste asked. 'But you must.'

Off an alley in the medina two archways side by side led into two tiled corridors, one for women, one for men.

The baths were like a cellar. Mortimer quickly heated up. The room was hot like a steam room, although only up above, under the vaulted roof, could you actually see steam drifting through the yellow light of dim bulbs. Around the wall brass taps trickled into stone basins. Men in undershorts sat cross-legged before them, scooping water over themselves. The trickling of the taps made a ringing music into which every so often came a slap as water hit the floor, a crash as someone rinsed themselves down, the boom of an empty bucket being set down.

The man at the door had given Mortimer a red plastic bowl and a packet of soap. He sat down beside a basin and poured bowl after bowl over himself. The water was not scalding but hot enough to cause a frisson each time. He watched a man soap up a lean-limbed boy of seven or eight, then rinse him down with bucketfuls, sending the white foam swirling across the floor in surf-lines. Mortimer did the same to himself.

He came out hot and dripping and sat on a tiled bench in a cool antechamber. From behind the iron door, which he had just closed with a long low boom, came the cymbal-crash of another bucketful landing on the floor, then the low murmur of a voice.

It seemed somehow right that this antechamber too be dim, as well as cool: a place to compose the senses before returning to the day. But there was more: a man in a grey jellaba conducted him to a high-ceilinged room jammed with cots. Mortimer lay down and the man covered him from head to toe in towels. He had been feeling a little chilly, and the fabric, though thin, gave just the warmth he needed. It was as if the entire process had been worked out over the ages so it exactly suited the human body. It was the ideal retreat and restoration.

He thought of Celeste, and realised all his good feeling about being here in the baths was really good feeling about her.

Afterwards, her hair straight and damp, her face a little ruddy, Celeste sat beside him quietly drinking mint tea at a café in a diminutive square in the medina, watching the bustle.

The petty commerce was fascinating. All you needed was a piece of torn plastic and an armful of fresh bright coriander, and you were in business. Across the street a boy opened a pack of cigarettes and set it on a box with the flip top open, selling them individually. Another boy had a bag of boiled eggs. For three dinars he'd rap one with his knuckles, peel the shell into his bag, pull out a big shaker and smother it with salt and cumin. Mortimer signalled to the boy and bought two. The yolk was perfect: smooth but not crumbly. Celeste hummed as she ate hers. Mortimer could not remember an egg tasting so good.

A man in a spiky-hooded burka walked past with a huge roll of rushes hanging from either shoulder. Mortimer couldn't think what they might be for, and indicated the figure to Celeste. She smiled and shrugged. A sad-looking man plodded along with two handfuls of dead chickens, as if weighed down by the guilty memory of having himself slit their throats that morning. Mule carts with motorcycle wheels came by every few minutes, laden with all manner of goods, their drivers sitting at the front with legs neatly crossed at the ankle.

There was something magnetic about the medina. If

you survived twenty-four hours in it, he had read somewhere, you would be hooked for ever. The dark alleys
snaking to right and left, and off them the cavernous
interiors, far more spacious than you'd expect, of the rug
sellers, their walls covered in the most subtle, persuasive
colours; and the leather stores, which you could pass blind-
folded and recognise by their luscious odour; and the
vegetables looking so healthy, as if the very plants pros-
pered in the soil of the Maghreb, under the extra care
farmers had to give them in this arid land: bulbous,
smooth-skinned potatoes, pale courgettes, giant pink
radishes white at their tips, crates of plump lettuces,
oranges in giant baskets strewn with their own dark leaves;
and the thick aroma of the spice sellers amid their heaps
of ochre, sienna, mustard and grey powders that lingered
in the nostrils long after you had passed them; and the
satisfying, well-machined clicking of the foot-powered
Singers in the many tailors' shops. And further away you'd
come to where the naked bloodless chickens hung by
yellow oversized feet from the doors of stalls, carcass after
pale carcass. On chopping blocks men axed necks with
large square blades, sliced off ankles, ripped out intestines.
And further still there'd be the stalls with the grey and
brown sponges of lungs, the plaits of grey-pink small intes-
tine, the long heavy droop of great white tongues with
their thick roots, and the wax-like folds of some other
stretch of innard hanging like misshapen tallow candles
from rusty hooks; and on tables in front, the shining
sprawls of full-grown liver shining like aubergine. The
gutters would be dark with blood, sticky under foot, with

a hard, thick smell in the air that you felt less in your nose than the back of the throat.

The one true purpose of a town or city was the exchange of goods. Here was human history: how to pass things around from one part to another. And who controlled their passage: were it not for moving things around, people would have stayed by their fields for ever, there'd never have been such a thing as a city.

Another boy brought them two brochettes, skewers two feet long with four chunks of grilled lamb on the end that had been marinated in some smoky spice.

Mortimer caught the rich sweet scent of hashish. Three tables away a group of men were deep in discussion, while creamy smoke billowed from under their table.

Earth and tiles: they went together so well. No designer could come up with anything as tasteful as this impoverished communal dwelling of a poor people.

Celeste blew steam off her glass of tea and said: 'It's lovely to us, but is it to them? They have so little. They probably wish it were different.'

'How much does one need?' Mortimer was surprised by a sense of great self-sufficiency.

'Still, it's not the same for them. We're lucky. We're here, you and me, for a little while. It all looks different, magical.'

He didn't like to think that one day in different circumstances it might strike him differently.

Then she said: 'You know that article you showed me? You're good at this. You shouldn't be wasted on news.'

'I like news.'

'I've seen a lot of journalists. They don't write like that.'

That remark would lodge in him in a way that was hard to swallow. Even years later it would sometimes unsettle him for a day or two at a time. Usually it would end with a big drinking session: a night of many beers, or Johnnie Walker, and he'd wake to a bright mist of hangover, and discover at last the discomfort gone, replaced by a headache.

'And the life is not all it's cracked up to be,' Celeste said. 'More and more, you just want to go home.'

But he found that hard to believe.

They sipped their tea. 'Well,' he said. 'I should be hitting the road. I mean, there is work to be done. Onwards and southwards.' He looked at her. 'Are you ready for that?'

Her eyes creased up in a smile, the green-blue irises seeming translucent as he looked into them. He saw something flinch deep within. 'But of course,' she said. 'What a question.'

8

The fat man had decided it would take him only two hours to drive Mortimer and Celeste to El Menia, the next town to the south, just as he had promised, come what may, no matter if conditions made it impossible, if landslides had blocked the road or if, as was the case, a savage khamsin was blowing. It was the darkest storm Mortimer had ever seen, and blew up just as they left Touggourt: first a thunderous darkness visible through the windscreen ahead, then a roaring black wind that enveloped the Peugeot.

They had met the fat man in a chicken restaurant, one of many cafés along the main street. He owned this particular one, as he had rapidly informed them in fluent, accented French. He wore slacks and a shirt open to the navel, and picked at a plate of greasy chicken wings as he asked them questions. Where were they going? What were they doing? He'd take them to El Menia next day. Yes, he was going there himself. And when they arrived they could stay with his friend Ben Youssef, who owned the largest store in El Menia. He wiped his hands on a towel.

For the excursion the fat man had looked up his favourite concubine, a chubby girl with problem skin inexpertly disguised with pancake make-up. She twisted round in the Peugeot's front seat, beaming at the foreigners, trying to engage them in conversation, heedless that her pasha was screaming down a dirt track at 120 kilometres per hour straight into a blanket of driving fog. Except it was worse than fog, it was like thick smoke, and poured across the road sending rivulets of dust sifting over the tarmac. Mortimer couldn't see how the man could make out the way ahead at all. Every so often he would jab the brakes, swerve, then accelerate again. Several times he had to really slam the brakes, and a pair of red lights would appear inches from the front bumper. Once, when the man stopped to pee and he stepped away from the car, he was instantly lost to view. Mortimer was surprised he could even find his way back to his door.

'Who is this maniac?' Celeste wanted to know. 'Tell him to slow down. *Dieu.*'

Mortimer tried, but the man only grinned back at him, resting a hand on his girlfriend's thigh, and offered some pleasantry that elicited gales of laughter from her, after which he tipped back his head and let out a long, delighted sigh.

Worse was to come. It turned out that the friend who owned the largest store in El Menia was actually an uncle, though he looked the same age, and he too had a concubine. They arrived around one o'clock, by which time the khamsin had blown itself out, leaving behind a day of consummate drabness. The red town brooded beneath a heavy sky of thick, dark cloud, dark such as presaged a thunderstorm, though there was little hope of that. A market was going on. It was the bleakest market Mortimer had ever seen: a few wrinkled tomatoes and limp white radishes. One trader had a sack of rice, half empty, the neck rolled down. Someone else was selling withered coriander. Mortimer made a half-hearted attempt to get away, find a hotel, or a lift on further south, but the day was too depressing, he couldn't muster the necessary persistence. Both Ben Youssef and his nephew the driver would have none of it. It was to be lunch with them, then the night. The following morning they would set up Mortimer and Celeste with a driver for Tamanrasset, their proper goal, still three long days away.

They ate lunch in a concrete room on a straw mat amid piles of boxes and crates. One wall was stacked high with large cans without labels. Mortimer wondered what they contained. Oil? Fruit? Meat? It was evidently a storeroom, but among all the stock, space had been cleared for cushions and rugs, and for the low table at which they sat. A local boy brought in a basket of dates. The two merchants reclined on their elbows, reaching out for the fruit. Then beers came (a bad sign here, Mortimer thought, after his pure days in the mountains: if they broke the alcohol precept who knew what others might follow), then dishes of stewed vegetables, fricasseed mutton, couscous, olives, fried potatoes. It was a spread. The concubines were thrilled, and fell upon the food vigorously. Which galvanised their men into sitting up, stuffing their thick thighs into cross-legged positions and commencing to gorge too. It was a lively scene: greasy fingers, greasy cheeks, and much slurping and belching. At first Mortimer was slightly appalled, and yearned to be alone with Celeste. In a way, he hated even to expose their love to the scene before them; or perhaps to be reminded that other kinds of love existed. The gluttony was so flagrant. But this was mid-desert, the land of paucity: no wonder they would fall on a feast. There was something almost biblical about it: not just the moral dubiousness of the scene, the graphic enactment of two deadly sins, but the sense of history, of merchants feasting like Old Testament kings in a land of nomads, dancing girls at their sides.

And Celeste didn't seem to mind; she ate and drank gratefully.

'So what brings you to the desert?' asked Ben Youssef, wiping his face with a towel.

Mortimer hesitated. It didn't seem right to arrive in a town and announce that he was a journalist. Before he knew it he might end up at the police station being asked to show his credentials and explain his presence. Algeria was nominally a free country, but muzzled by religion on the one hand and socialism on the other. Foreign journalists would hardly be regular visitors down here. He shrugged and said, 'Tourism.' The word sounded unconvincing even to his own ears.

Youssef leaned to one side and brushed the opposite knee, smoothing his robe. 'Your friend has nice cameras. Must be worth a lot of money.' He eyed Celeste appraisingly.

'She likes to take photographs,' Mortimer said.

Celeste frowned at him.

The man hadn't shaved in a while. His cheeks were smooth and round, but speckled with sparse little bristles. He asked, 'What is your particular interest? The ancient sites of the desert?'

Mortimer nodded. He knew there were rock carvings in the hills near Tamanrasset which tourists visited. He added, 'And the Tuareg, of course.'

He felt uneasy. He would much prefer to have been open. Ben Youssef was a fine example of the Arab merchant, well fed, legs almost too chubby to cross, living amid his multifarious stock. He was a proper man of the world. Mortimer imagined he might strike up an easy rapport with a man like that, who would know the value of publicity.

Youssef said something to his nephew, and both men laughed. Then, addressing one of his knees, he announced: 'But if you're interested in the Tuareg, you should go to Timimoun. Perhaps you'll be able to tell us what the

Tuareg are doing there. They don't belong round here, as you know.'

'Timimoun?'

'Two hundred kilometres west of here. But surely you have a map?'

In fact, he didn't have a map. Within Algeria there were no maps of Algeria, except for the featureless colour mosaics on schoolroom walls.

'Of course,' Mortimer said: anything not to arouse suspicion. 'But I don't understand, are Tuareg settling in Timimoun?'

'Tuareg settle nowhere. They are gathering there, so one hears. Or near there. They don't like to come into a town. Anyway.' Ben Youssef clapped, like some old sheikh. 'Time for cognac.'

It crossed Mortimer's mind that this might be a lead worth pursuing, but when the story about the Tuareg, if there was one, was anyway so amorphous, and when the heart of Tuareg territory was unquestionably Tamanrasset, right in the middle of the desert, still three days away, and when moreover travel in these parts was hardly easy – either finding a lift, or the state of the pistes, could potentially turn a twenty-mile journey into a matter of many hours – the idea of going to Timimoun registered only a flicker of a possibility in his mind. They'd do better to sit tight, let these two local bigwigs show off to them some more, then get sent on their way south with, hopefully, a reliable driver. At least this was a country where if a man could, he looked after a stranger. The local hospitality seemed so natural, in fact, that it struck Mortimer as odd that in the West such an ancient human practice, celebrated by Homer, long-established by biblical times, should have been so thoroughly lost.

As it turned out, chance was on their side. Just as the boy arrived to answer Ben Youssef's clap for the brandy, there came a rapping on another door. It opened to reveal a young man with his head wrapped in a scarf. He was one of Ben Youssef's shop assistants, and needed a German speaker to interpret for him. He apparently knew his boss was entertaining foreigners, and had come to see if one of them could help. Mortimer offered, even though he had only a smattering of German, and was led down a dark corridor into another storeroom, and from the far end of that into the back of a shop. The two German medics he'd seen in Touggourt were standing at the counter.

'We are trying to buy two jerrycans,' they told him. 'We are thinking better to have more water and gasoline.'

'*Jerry*,' Mortimer explained to the shop assistant. '*Deux*.' And to the Germans: 'No chance of a lift out of here, I suppose? Two people, two bags? Well, three bags.' The third being Celeste's camera bag.

Then it was a matter of setting the refrain going and sticking to it: 'We are leaving with our friends. We have found our friends. *Nous partons avec nos amis*.'

As Mortimer had anticipated, the two merchants were none too happy about losing their afternoon's entertainment. 'But you must let us organise everything,' they insisted. At least they still had their concubines to amuse them.

Then once Mortimer and Celeste had settled themselves and their bags in the VW van, the Germans decided
it was too late in the day to set off. Instead, they parked
up in the town's desolate '*Camping*', an empty lot enclosed
by a red perimeter wall, that must have been installed
back in the sixties, when the great southern highway was
built, the highway that already, a decade on, was so
potholed and heat-shattered that traffic preferred to
meander along the old pistes that still ran beside it.

The Germans went off for a walk round town, leaving
Mortimer and Celeste alone in the van.

They shut the orange curtains around the windows and
folded down the benches to make up the small double
bed, then spread out two thick blankets. All at once in
the red-hued interior it was as if they were once again
quite alone, and the world had retreated.

As they lay together she told him about her family.
When she was sixteen, her father had taught her to sail
at their holiday home north of Bordeaux. She'd had her
own dinghy for scuttling around the harbour. Her father
was dead now. Her mother, now in her sixties, lived in
Pau, in the foothills of the Pyrenees, kept busy by her
younger sister who though only twenty-seven already had
four children. She was married to a baker who owned
three *boulangeries* in the area. 'They both drive new
Citroëns.' She shrugged and smiled. 'And what about you?'

'Tell me more,' he said. 'Your brother, your uncles and
aunts, grandparents, nephews, nieces.'

She was pleased, enjoying herself, and lay propped on an
elbow as she went through her family album. He found it

fascinating to hear about them, as if he was being introduced to the cast of a film he knew he was about to enjoy.

Her younger brother was troubled. He was bright, but had dropped out of the Sorbonne and now no one was sure what he was doing in Paris.

She closed her eyes and kissed him. Mortimer told her he had never expected to have an experience like this.

'I expected it,' she said. 'But it never exactly happened so I stopped expecting it.'

Then she frowned and rolled off him. 'Maybe this is the Eden from which one must be thrown out.'

He didn't know what to say. He felt he wouldn't mind even if it turned out to be true, as long as she was with him.

She asked about Saskia.

When he thought about Saskia now, there seemed nothing fearful or doom-laden about the two and a half years he'd been with her, nor even about the wrench of breaking it off. He no longer felt guilty, it already seemed part of his history that could not have happened differently.

Celeste was interested in her: how had they met, where had they lived, where did she work, what was she like.

'She's serious,' he said.

'Like you too,' Celeste said with a smile. 'You're a serious man.'

'Am I?'

She screwed up her face in a smile. 'I like that.'

He thought for a moment. 'Saskia's a moral person. I mean, she was more political than me. I remember once telling her she was too moral for me. And she said: "I'm too moral for you? You ought to think about that.'"

At the time he'd experienced a plunge of guilt. But now he thought that even if Saskia had been right to upbraid him, still there had been no cause for alarm. All things were possible. If he needed to adjust his attitudes, he could do that.

'I was engaged once too,' Celeste told him. 'Sort of. We never actually told anyone.'

'Who was he?'

'A psychiatrist. He worked at the hospital.'

'What happened?'

'I wasn't ready to be tied down.'

'Was that all?'

An answer caught in her throat. Then she said, 'It's always more complicated. The timing was wrong. Some things were good, and right, but it wasn't going to work then, and it didn't. I didn't want it as much as I thought. You have to really *want* it. You know?'

Mortimer was silent. 'What was he called?'

'What does it matter?' she said. Then thought better of it, and said, 'Eric,' pronouncing it the French way, and shrugged. '*Eric*,' she repeated with a sigh.

It was different in different languages: *je t'aime* produced a flurry of feeling like an adolescent crush. *I love you* released a serious, grown-up sensation, full of importance. *Ich liebe dich* was exciting, with its wartime associations, the sense of being engaged with an alien power. *Ya tebya lyublyu* with its comic bundle of labials could be counted on to raise a laugh, and more often than not led to sex. But then in the throes of lovemaking, if they said it again it was deadly serious, and changed the way you felt about death. As she spread her knees under his arms, and he laid his forearms along the inside of her calves and closed his hands around the chamois-like soles of her feet, he would say it once more, only this time he would no longer be sure which was his own language.

Celeste and Mortimer wandered around a development on the edge of the town, a broad new avenue of red cement houses without roofs or windows, with kerbs for imaginary pavements and rows of bare poles that would one day be street lamps. It was a brand new ghost town. Yet already it looked down-at-heel, tatty, neglected. Other than one sheet of dusty plastic crackling in the breeze there were none of the usual signs of an active building site, no parked diggers or cement mixers, no wheelbarrows or shovels even, no stacks of bricks and blocks. It was as if the scheme had run out of money, or of will. Whorls of red dust skittered over the empty road.

This must all have been part of the government's Saharan initiative. Mortimer had heard that they had started building new towns along the southern highway. Algeria had for a long time been looking for a way to yoke the Sahara into its economy. Seismologists had been working to establish the most viable mines, natural gas they had already found, and a plan had been drawn up for a pipeline that would run north to the coastal city of Oran. There was a rumour of oil reserves. They had apparently decided they must go ahead regardless, and take advantage of the space the desert offered. New towns, new roads, persuasive incentives for people to move: if they could only get a critical mass of population down into the desert, they'd start reaping the rewards. The Sahara was their Wyoming, their territory west of the Mississippi: it was just a matter of inducing the prospectors, the entrepreneurs and homesteaders to make the leap.

It was strange to see a boy come down the empty street on a donkey, under the bare posts. But quickly it was the boy on the donkey who seemed ordinary, and the hollow shells of the cement houses extraordinary.

Mortimer and Celeste passed an uncomfortable night curled up in the camper van.

Mortimer loved it. This was how he loved life: an endless relay of new people, himself the baton passed from hand to hand. It seemed the ideal way to live.

9

When Mortimer awoke the next morning he could hear a discussion in German going on outside. He parted the minivan's thin curtains. A smoky desert dawn, the hiss of a camping stove. Mortimer sat up and rubbed his face, pushed the blanket off his legs reluctantly: he had grown cold in the night. The door of the van whined as he slid it back on its runners.

The Germans had spent the night in their large orange tent. They were standing now in sandals looking away towards the red wall of the campsite. They finally concluded their discussions and delivered the bombshell. It was a small bombshell: after all, they were not going south but west. They had decided to visit a clinic staffed by some Egyptian doctors they'd met at a conference the year before.

'Where exactly?' Mortimer asked.

'Timimoun.'

Theirs was the only vehicle in the campsite. Mortimer bowed to fate. He climbed back into the van with the news.

Celeste was lying on her side propped on an arm. She brushed a lock from her face. 'I heard.' She frowned. She had a way of frowning before summoning something from deep within. What she summoned now was optimism. She said: 'But that's great. We can go to Timimoun.'

She opened her school map of the country over her legs. He settled beside her. Her body was warm. He could feel that she was happy. He was happy too: to be free and travelling, with a potentially terrific story ahead of him to which he need not hurry, there being no one else likely to be on its trail — the world cared little about the Sahara at the best of times — to be in this easy mobile state with a woman it suited equally well seemed a triumph, a fulfilment.

'What's so good about that?' he asked.

'It's perfect,' she said. 'We can check out these Tuareg who are supposedly gathering at Timimoun. Why not? And there are ksars around there, big mud forts. Library wanted me to get some pictures of them.'

What it meant, in a nutshell, was that instead of going where Mortimer needed to go, the Germans were going where Celeste wanted to go. It was true, undeniably, that she could work in many places. You never knew where the classic shot might be taken. But she had pencilled Timimoun into her itinerary, apparently. And Mortimer felt good about it, a warmth kindled in his midriff: he could wish good for her without it costing him a thing. Quite the reverse, it gave him something in return.

Five straight hours down a decent track, a late instalment of the Saharan investment, and they were at Timimoun. Mortimer would never have guessed then that they were heading to the heart of the story.

The Egyptian doctors in Timimoun were not happy men. When they had signed up for their eighteen-month stints down here, they hadn't realised the sizeable salaries they would receive in return for bringing the light of modern medicine into the darkest, blindingest Sahara would be paid in Algerian dinars, a non-exchangeable currency. They would leave the country with nothing. And there was nothing to spend their dinars on in Timimoun.

They represented a last ghost of a link to the modern world. There were five of them, and they lived in two new houses, the bleakest Mortimer had yet seen. Like the doctors themselves, the houses were part of the Saharan initiative. The government had constructed a compound of concrete homes outside Timimoun's old town walls, with plumbing, electricity, gas cookers and baths. But the town seldom had electricity, its water often failed to arrive for days, and it had never had gas, so whoever lived in these houses did so in squalor far beneath the humblest

Saharan home. So far only the Egyptians' two houses were occupied. The Germans were put up in one, Mortimer and Celeste in the other. The kitchen was impenetrably clogged with filthy pans. The doctors had given up going into it, preferring to cook on a fire outside. The bathroom stank. In the bathtub a large blue barrel stood under the tap, half filled with brown water. The tap was left permanently on: they had to catch the water whenever it happened to arrive.

The doctors gratefully changed money with Mortimer at an inflated rate, which neither side was supposed to do. Celeste felt sorry for them, in spite of the dark, lascivious glances they couldn't help casting her way, and changed more money than she would ever be able to get rid of.

One of them, a Copt called Mansour, was content. He dressed in a white kaftan and had a bushy moustache in his otherwise clean-shaven, shiny, bronze face. He might have been fifty, was a good size, well fed, and moved in a sleek and graceful manner.

'It's a special experience,' Mansour told Mortimer, 'to live in the heart of the largest desert.'

He couldn't understand why his colleagues refused to resign themselves to it. He went for walks beside the town's red walls in the evening, when the heat was bearable, and played a lot of chess, gathering up his white robe and settling on a cushion with a sigh of satisfaction before a fresh board. He was good at it. Mortimer played several games with him and lost them all.

The desert light was sharp and clear around Timimoun. You'd see the sheet of land glinting away to distant hills, tinged blue in the morning, mauve and suave in the evening. The hills were smooth as porcelain on the skyline. Why did it always seem a time of healing just to be in a desert? Mortimer wondered. What was it in one that seemed to recover, find its feet again? He could already feel the desert working its magic on him.

Each time Mortimer attempted to get inside the walls of the old town, he was conducted to the same bare mud room with a hole in its roof, where he was left alone until sooner or later a man could be found to sit with the guest. There'd be a glass of tea, a munch of dates, and a lot of silence; then he'd be dismissed, escorted back to the gates. There was no question of a guided tour. The town was in the middle of some protracted festivity that forbade visitors.

The town gate itself consisted of a Moorish arch thirty feet tall built into the mud walls, and within it two tall wooden doors, each made of a patchwork of boards, elaborately carved and patterned, stained near-black by centuries of sun and dust. Some were set with designs of iron studs. It was as if wood had been made to resemble a local patchwork of rugs.

At night drums played behind the old walls. Mortimer longed to know why, to witness whatever ceremony was in progress, but it was Celeste who got to see it. The event was women-only, some rite of passage for the town nubiles. She came back late one night with her eyes glazed with excitement and her hair done up in a network of plaits. The women had made her up with henna and oil that made her face glisten, then taught her their hip-rolling dance. She couldn't believe how sexual the dance was. 'Those women have a fine old time behind closed doors,' she said. They'd let her take photographs too.

Mortimer felt pleased. Her evening inside the town gates underlined that this trip was good for her too. If anything, there was a pique that she had successfully penetrated the old town, and he hadn't. Except that feeling quickly transmuted into a satisfaction on her behalf, as if anything she gained was also a gain for him.

They spent three days here nominally achieving nothing; yet Mortimer didn't mind. He was a free agent, just as he had always wanted. Hiatuses were inevitable. They were good, they allowed a little mental digestion to take place. They had a barometric value. He told himself that when once more he ventured in pursuit of the elusive quarry he would have an extra layer of awareness.

When the drums stopped late at night Mortimer could hear camels bellowing and rumbling. Once he saw a Tuareg, unmistakably, a tall man in black wearing a high black headpiece wandering off to the west on a camel with two asses in his wake.

Mansour confirmed that now and then Tuareg did pass through, and there had been a number in the town lately. But they had all headed into the sands to the west, probably to trade in the chain of oases a few hours' walk away. Mortimer and Celeste decided that since they were here, they would go at least to the nearest of these oases, where Celeste could photograph one of the mud forts: all the villages in the region had ksars. And they might possibly find some Tuareg to interview too.

Mansour introduced them to an ancient, wiry guide called Brahim, and arranged the first leg of their journey: four hours to the oasis of Tessalit.

On their last evening Mansour cooked them a chickpea stew, and they drank numerous small pots of tea.

'The desert is good for a man because there he meets God face to face,' Mansour averred. 'God loves the desert. It is the one place He left empty, just for Himself. But you must be careful. Go nowhere without the guide. Even a village one hour away, it is easy to miss. And if you miss it –' He shrugged, opened his palms.

There was presumably always the consolation that even if one did lose one's way, one would already be in the arms of God, the desert being His private garden.

There was a kind of half-avenue along the town wall, one single row of royal palms, splendidly tall, their crowns tossing like flags in the breeze, their trunks painted white to head height, giving them a tame, French aspect. Mortimer and Celeste had a strange moment along this avenue the night before they left.

A crescent moon was up: it was not long after sunset. By now Mortimer felt the desert truly inside him: a powdery taste to his saliva, a wonderful chalky feeling in his limbs.

Lately he had been asking himself why he always exaggerated things. Love, for example: either it was the one terminal love for which he had been made and destined since birth, or else, as with Saskia, a thorough and deplorable compromise. Why couldn't it be a simple matter of pleasure and enjoyment?

Under those half-painted, half-moonlit palms, with the desert silence stretching off into ineffability, he had felt compelled to force the issue with Celeste. He had thought he wanted to be sure it really was the same for her, that she also had never felt like this before, and so on; but perhaps he had merely been trying to pass the load on to her: she could carry the great love for a while.

Just then he'd have been better off not asking. Before asking, it was clear she felt as he did. After, less so. Perhaps she indeed felt that this might be the love of her life, until that very moment of weakness, when he tried to check. At which point, a faint question mark was pencilled in the margin by his name. That was how he would think of it much later, though at the time he soon brushed the thought aside: it was a mistake to ponder things too deeply.

He had expected her to answer his question with a smile, a hug, a kiss. Instead, she kept staring out over the flat plain, and said: 'What matters, all that matters, is deciding what you want. That is everything.'

10

They set out before dawn. Brahim, the guide, was waiting by the town gates with a ruffled little donkey. They walked along the road a while in the morning chill. Mortimer was pleased when they branched off on to a white path through rubble – perhaps a former house, or midden – and it led them into sunlight. Immediately the warmth felt good on his legs, the coldest part of him. The very first rays of the sun were peering over the lip of the flat earth.

The plain was a sheet of perfectly smooth plaster. Traces of salt showed here and there as white blemishes, and occasional coruscations of diminutive rubble had been glazed into the surface. The ground might once have been mud, Mortimer thought, perhaps part of the ocean-bed the Sahara had been. It was a marvellous pavement for walking on. It was remarkable how natural things could look so man-made. At that hour, with the sun just up and warming the traveller's night-chilled limbs, it was a wonderful thing to be walking on such a surface.

It wasn't long before Mortimer had removed his sweater and draped it over his shoulders. Then that seemed too warm and he tied it round his waist. He was glad he had a hat. Then it began to be seriously hot. He undid the buttons of his shirt, reluctant to take it off in case his arms burned.

Celeste's face shone, with sweat, with heat, with the brightness of the day, and with what looked like happy surprise. But actually she wasn't happy. She hadn't slept well and her period had arrived in the night. There was some relief it had arrived at all, but mostly it was despicably inconvenient, as she said. How was she to go about dealing with it mid-march?

Early in the hike Mortimer said, thinking aloud: 'I've never been on a job that felt so good. The Amazon Indians have one word that means both work and play. This is it.' He turned to grin at her. That was when she told him about the sanitary problem.

After a moment, she said, 'You know, I've been doing photojournalism for nine years already. One starts thinking about not becoming a lonely, leathery woman who is at home nowhere.'

'Or at home everywhere. That's the best, surely.'

'No. It's more or less the same anyway.'

'What about the Tuareg? They live nowhere.'

'They know where they belong. They have somewhere they belong. We all do.'

He fell silent, listened to their footfalls on the smooth clay, a pleasant light sound in the warmth of dawn and the fresh new light. He couldn't quite believe what she was saying, that she really thought it. Maybe one day it would be right to settle. But when there was the whole world waiting?

They were halfway across the plain before Mortimer realised the far hills he had been seeing from Timimoun were not hills at all, but sand dunes. From a distance they had taken on the usual colours of hills – brown, blue, even green – but now, a mile or so off, they were a uniform orange. They formed part of the world's biggest ocean of sand, the Grand Erg, every schoolboy's vision of the desert, Saint-Exupéry's trial by fire, Père Foucauld's house of God, his burning bush. This was where they were going.

They hadn't even reached the sand when it became clear that Brahim was getting on Celeste's nerves. His donkey carried two large sacks, one of onions, one of oranges, on top of which sat Mortimer's and her bags. A rope was looped over the animal's rump, and Brahim decided that

Celeste should hold it. She didn't want to. Brahim was insistent. Again and again he took her hand and placed it on the rope, only to have her let go a few steps later.

'Why does he want me to hold this stupid strap?' she eventually blurted out. Then: '*Non!*' directed at Brahim.

Part of the problem was their lack of Arabic, Brahim's of French. But also there was something undeniably chattel-like about the position he wanted Celeste to adopt. Mortimer could understand her reluctance to be attached physically to their little caravan, quite apart from its interfering with her stride. Mortimer could imagine that had he himself not been there, Brahim would have got out a rope and tied her to the animal. Mortimer shrugged at Brahim non-committally, meaning either: Ah well, what can you do? Or else: What is the purpose of your desire to have her hold on? He felt he ought to intervene before any serious ill feeling developed. This wiry old man would soon be their only lifeline.

By way of reply Brahim made a fist and jabbed it forwards. Mortimer took it to mean that she wasn't walking fast enough. He hadn't noticed, nor could he imagine how Brahim had, for they hadn't been walking long, and Celeste hadn't been falling behind. But Brahim turned out to have been prophetic.

The dunes never seemed to get any closer.

By the time they arrived at the foot of the first slope, Mortimer had more or less forgotten that the dunes were their initial goal. He was just a man walking across a plain under the sun, his mind blank. Two hours had passed. Mortimer was hot now, though not sweaty. It was supposed to take four hours in all to the village of Tessalit, and he tried to ask Brahim if it was two hours more from here. '*Encore deux heures?*' he said a few times, holding up two fingers.

Brahim cracked a smile and said something in Arabic. His face was not so much lined as folded into deep wrinkles that became even deeper when he smiled. Then he said, '*Quat' heures.*' The same four-hour story. It was disconcerting. It was possible he had understood Mortimer's question, and they still had four hours to go. People might consider the four-hour trek to begin once you reached the dunes, the plain being just a preamble.

Celeste was having a hard time now. '*Excusez-moi,*' she said, stumbling up the sand and disappearing over the nearest brow.

It was very quiet: just a rustling from where Celeste had gone. The donkey flicked its ears. Mortimer had a vague idea that he should try and appreciate the stillness, the silence, the expanse, but one couldn't do something like that while walking in the desert: it was too hot, the sun was too strong. It beat down on one's head giving no respite for contemplation. The important thing was to keep moving, to get across.

There was something drab about the sand. There it stood in an enormous heap. A few trails of dust led off on to the pan of the plain. It was like a building site: the cement beneath one's feet, the heap of sand waiting to find a use.

Brahim kept looking up the dune Celeste had climbed. Mortimer assumed it was a reflex of prurience, until he started muttering, '*Yalah, yalah,*' under his breath: Let's go.

The rustling stopped. Silence. Then Celeste appeared at the top of the slope, and waded down towards them.

Brahim gave up on his bid to have her hold on to the donkey. They settled on a compromise: she agreed to allow the donkey to carry her camera bag, but only once it had been tied on to her satisfaction.

They had brought six litres of Sidi Ali, surely enough water for a four-hour walk. But four litres were already gone.

Brahim went barefoot. Mortimer could see why. It was hard enough wading up a sand dune, but doing it in a pair of heavy boots was gruelling. Brahim walked lightly, he seemed to skip over the sand, hardly sinking in. That was clearly the way to do it, but Mortimer didn't see how one could in a pair of boots. After they had scaled the second dune he took his boots off. Which was fine on the shady side of a dune, but alarming on the sunny, until he learned to accept the fierce tingle of the scalding sand. It wasn't exactly pain, and it made one walk faster, energised the limbs.

At the fourth dune things began to change. This one was three or four hundred feet tall, a monster. Brahim led them up diagonally, doubtless a good idea, but Mortimer found himself longing for just one level pace. It went on too long, having to plod with the right leg always plunging down, throwing the stride off kilter. Celeste was conspicuously lagging by the time they reached the crest. She paused when she was still thirty yards below them: a few minutes' worth of slogging. She stopped because they stopped.

The scene that greeted Mortimer from that first high ridge was of hundreds of still more enormous dunes folding away into the distance, a mountain range of sand. But the biggest surprise was when he looked back: the plain of Timimoun had vanished. All he could see was dunes, in every direction. '*Mais où est Timimoun?*' he asked.

Brahim looked up from feeding the donkey an orange.

'Timimoun?' Mortimer repeated.

Brahim pointed out a short dark line just showing between the brows of two dunes. What was it? The top of the town wall? Part of the plain?

Brahim cut another orange and gave half to Mortimer. He gestured towards Celeste with the other half. But she wasn't moving. She had sat down. Brahim called out. She was too tired even to look up. Reluctantly, Mortimer stumbled down towards her.

She had her head in her hands. She shook her head when he came close. 'I'm all right,' she said. 'Just a bit dizzy. *C'est rien*. It'll pass.'

Brahim called down again, gesturing that Mortimer should get her to her feet. He put a hand under her shoulder. 'He thinks you should stand up.'

She shook her head again, but eventually accepted the need to carry on, and stumbled up the slope.

Brahim gave Celeste the half-orange. She didn't want it. He insisted, making a mime of eating. She obliged, frowning. The frown went away at the first bite. Juice ran over her fingers, down her chin. Mortimer felt pleased that she was now enjoying the same experience he had a moment ago. He had never known an orange taste so good. She turned the skin inside out and gnawed it, then Brahim took it off her and fed it to the donkey.

A fly buzzed into Mortimer's hair. He brushed it away reflexively, then thought: Where did that fly come from? Either it somehow managed to live amid these piles of sand, or it came along for the ride with the donkey. In which case it had better not lose them. He imagined it buzzing over the dunes in search of its human ferry across the emptiness. It was the only living thing they encountered that day.

Brahim rearranged the donkey's load, and created a two-foot end of rope extending from beneath the pack. He insisted that Celeste hold it, and more than hold. He wound it round her wrist and put the end in her palm, so as she gripped it, it gripped her.

As he stood waiting for Brahim to fasten Celeste to the beast Mortimer was overcome by a wave not of fatigue but sleepiness. His body was primed and pumped for exertion, yet he could have nodded off standing up. It was disconcerting.

Twice Celeste untied herself and Brahim did her up again. Mortimer didn't try to intervene.

After yearning to stop, to rest, for the walk to be over, Mortimer fell into a kind of trance. There was nothing for it but to forget the painful necessity of putting one foot in front of the other, one step always higher or lower than the next, always slipping in the sand, and just keep doing it, until the mind lost all but the remotest awareness of what the body was doing. Up, down, up, down, shush-shush. The donkey was good to have along, not only because it carried things, but as a pace-setter. You couldn't get it to go slower or faster, and you stopped it at your peril. After the long halt for oranges Brahim had quite a time slapping and exhorting it to set off again. And then it was exemplary. It simply bowed its head and kept going. It was clear one must do the same, and the beast showed how.

Except the mind didn't exactly become unaware of the body. In a way it grew more aware. It was as if Mortimer slipped through the desire to stop, and arrived in a land where all things were clearer and more illuminated, but there was no desire here, one accepted everything as it was.

Celeste was silent. When Mortimer looked at her she seemed to have given up all will. Her right arm extended towards the animal's rump, and she shuffled along behind it, oblivious. Mortimer wondered if she too was learning from the donkey. Not to think, not to notice, just to keep on with no thought for where one was going.

The soles of Mortimer's feet began to itch. Every step became a way of scratching them. It felt good to sink one's feet grindingly into the grains. He wondered if perhaps he ought to stop and investigate, but he didn't want to risk either breaking his semi-trance, or finding that all was not well with his feet. He could imagine the skin utterly dried out, cracking under the pressure of the dry particles.

The deep troughs between the dunes became gulfs of darkness. It was odd that they should be so dark. As the sun climbed it ought to have illuminated them more. Mortimer looked for the sun. It wasn't where it ought to have been: not high overhead but quite low. Its light was rich, orange, palpable.

Celeste was now manifestly being dragged by the donkey. She stumbled along behind it, her arm outstretched. She was wearing a pair of Mortimer's shorts on her head, from beneath which her hair hung lank. Her face was pink, shining.

When she tried to drink, Brahim took the bottle away and gave her another orange. Once, they stopped high on a crest. Tremendous mountains rose ahead of them, carved by the sun into slopes and gulfs of shadow. They were a magnificent sight, a range of gold. It seemed a sight not intended for human eyes.

The sand under his feet turned to gold, and it seemed that the whole landscape was made of gold, suffused with gold light. It was like catching a glimpse of a heaven, of one of the realms notated in the margins of the Koran. Like walking a land above the earth. They had in fact been steadily climbing. Behind, Mortimer thought he could make out a hazy patch that might have been the plain of Timimoun, visible once again because they were high enough. Brahim indicated with a downward gesture that they would soon be travelling downhill. It seemed that they communicated more easily now, as if they had broken into a world where they could recognise and understand one another. Mortimer felt like he was on stage, under the gaze of people above.

He experienced intense waves of love towards Celeste.

He thought of putting an arm round her, giving her a kiss. It was unnecessary. She was there too, standing on the same orange stage. The waves of feeling detached themselves from any object. They came by themselves. Just to be standing here was a pleasure, a wonder. He was no longer afraid of having to carry on. He could stop, start, climb, descend, look around, with every movement somehow abundantly simple, as if he'd been liberated from a heavy load.

Now he couldn't think of their destination. There was no destination; it had evaporated like a mirage. There was just the walking, and the world of sand all around. There was nowhere to be but right here where they were. The gold and rust-brown slopes seemed to infiltrate his body, as if he were not looking out at the world, but somehow had entered the world, or the world had entered him. Every time he recognised that their destination had been snuffed out, more waves of warm feeling washed through him. Wakefulness, which was a kind of love, burned in him like a watchfire.

The donkey snorted, blew through its lips. They all ate another orange, which tasted miraculous to Mortimer, sweet and rich, then they gave the animal the husks, which it ate noisily, not minding when one of them fell, acquiring a coating of sand: he plucked it up, ate it anyway.

It might have been in another hour or two, as the sun was getting close to the horizon, that they saw land again. First a smoky red cliff, then a long dark line among the dunes. Brahim said the line was a palm garden. Then a tremendous red fortress appeared, perched halfway up the red cliff: a castle out of fable, missable at first, so closely did its colour match the clay around it, of which it was made. It looked so old and legendary that it could only have been a ruin. Then they were on the last slope of sand, could actually see a track below, pale in the gathering dark. It crossed Mortimer's mind that he should put his boots on. But he couldn't remember where they were, and anyway night was falling, they were walking through blue air now, and already a lone palm stood ahead, and beyond it he could see a dark geometry of more palms, an orchard, a forest of trees, and a dog was barking somewhere. The donkey bellowed as it walked, its head stooped, ears folded right back, then it swivelled its ears forwards. Far away a wheezing started that worked itself into a bray and came echoing back at them. Then they were walking beside a little earthen dyke, and they were under palms now, in a dark avenue of still trees. The fronds glistened overhead. The track ran in two parallel paths, pale in the darkness, just as if vehicles used it, which plainly they couldn't do. No vehicle could cross those dunes. The dust was pleasantly packed, smooth under foot. There was no need for boots. It would have been centuries of bare feet and hoofs that made it that way. Faint stripes lay across it: moon-shadows of the palms. Once Mortimer felt a prick in his right foot but it didn't come back, and soon they were approaching the goal. Mortimer didn't know what it was at first. He thought there was a tiled patio up ahead, implausibly laid out among the trees. But the donkey recognised it, and plodded straight towards it, lowering its neck. Even when it touched its lip to the dark surface and sent a ring of light travelling over it, Mortimer still didn't immediately recognise what it was. Once he did, instead of relief he felt a strange disappointment, unease, a mild nausea.

I I

Mortimer woke to find himself lying in a room of bare earth with sand for a floor. It was cool sand, fine and clean. In the roof was a square hole, and through that a sky too bright to look at. A rectangle of white sunlight lay on the floor like a rug, one corner of it folding up on to the wall. It was a marvellous room, one felt safe in it. Why didn't everyone build like this?

Someone had thrown a blanket over him, and his head rested on a cushion. He sat up and realised a fly was sitting on his nose. Another person lay nearby. At first, oddly, he thought: Saskia. Then the tousled blonde hair reminded him. He put his hand on Celeste's hip, let it rest there. No response. She was fast asleep. He could feel her slow breaths.

What time must it be? His legs ached. When he attempted to stand, pain stabbed the soles of his feet. He slumped to the floor gasping. When the shock had subsided, he pulled off a sock and inspected the sole. It was an awful sight. A maze of red crevasses criss-crossed the skin, some of them quarter of an inch deep. It was ghastly to look at, though the pain had already subsided. After the deep sleep he had been in, he was too dreamy to feel anything other than curiosity: what would happen now that his feet were unwalkable? He had a few Band-Aids, a tub of Vaseline somewhere, and an old tube of Savlon knocking around in a side pocket of his bag, but they weren't up to this.

He put the sock back on, introducing it gently to the skin. The gashes didn't hurt. The material tickled, that was all. He sat back against the rough wall, relieved that at least he wouldn't be walking anywhere soon: he wouldn't be able to.

The air in the room felt thick with desert light, with peace, with sanctity. Why didn't people back home decorate their rooms like this? All you needed was earth, sand, and a rug of sunlight, half of it spread on the floor, the rest hanging on the wall. He felt he had stumbled into a sanctuary from the troubled, corrupted world, the world that did not have the heart to cross thousands of miles of desert.

Celeste's hair lay over her face. The sunlight picked out a few strands and turned them into a tangle of gold filaments. The morning sun, the quiet room made of earth, the beauty asleep with her hair just touched by the sun, her warm body wrapped in a blanket of rough black wool: a flush of feeling swept into him: they had made it. Yesterday had been an ordeal. So much so that he had even forgotten their arrival at this village, wherever it was. Then he remembered: Tessalit, first oasis out of Timimoun, in the Great Western Erg. And he vaguely recollected the first sight of the ksar, a tower of clay among the palms, which he'd taken to be some outcrop of rock until he saw the dark doorway at the foot of it. That must be where they were now, somewhere deep inside it.

He began to feel wonderfully clear-headed, and rummaged in his bag for his notebook. When he stood up again his legs trembled and threatened to crumple, and he quickly settled on the cool sand floor.

Tessalit

What the hell am I doing? I love this. A whisker of purpose, and otherwise I'm tossing myself on the waves. Waves of sand, presumably. I mean, there's going to be a story somewhere, for sure, but in a little oasis in the middle of nowhere? On the other hand, we are digressively on our way south. In other words, towards: 1. Tamanrasset, where I'll try and find Señor El Kebir, the Mr Big, the Tuareg leader. Assuming there is one, and I can get myself pointed to him. 2. The Malian border villages, where the drought is said to be worst: the edge of the Sahel. Once the Sahel, now just more Sahara. Two sure-fire stories. (What the hell does Sahara mean anyway?) But that can all wait. For now it's too much just to be here in this medieval keep made of mud in the middle of the desert. With Celeste.

He clipped his pen in the breast pocket of his shirt and steered himself across the floor on his knees. What a good floor sand made: you could lie or sit with equal comfort, and it even smelled good.

He planted a long kiss on Celeste's cheek. She drew in a slow breath, stretched an arm, then hummed, '*C'est bien, c'est bien.'* A shudder ran through her and she fell asleep again.

His belly tightened. This was the woman for him: the idea arrived as a discovered certainty. It seemed obvious that all along he had been destined to end up with a gutsy Continental photographer from the Pyrenees, with golden skin and a couple of SLRs and her own agenda, from which nothing would deflect her, certainly not him. This was a real relationship, not the dark tomb in which most couples agreed to bury themselves. I'll go in if you go in, oh all right then, now let's close the door and wait till we die. What kind of life was that? The biggest notions in life were the biggest lies. To shut yourself up with the same person in some half-asleep life: it was how most people ended up wasting their precious days. Love was the biggest device known to mankind to speed the passage of decades, to rip the heart out of a life.

But this was something else: love like gasoline, that fuelled you in your own life, didn't demand you make impossible choices.

But he did need to get to where the action was, and before too long. A couple of days out here, she taking her snaps, then back on the road to Tamanrasset, to the Tuareg resistance. It wouldn't do to miss out on anything when he was so close. But he had a strange confidence that nothing would happen until he got there, as if he himself might be the catalyst the situation awaited. Whatever the situation was; if only he knew more.

Mortimer touched Celeste's hip and again she shuddered alarmingly. It was as if her body sensed the touch but didn't recognise him, and jolted in shock. Then she lay still, breathing silently. He felt her side rise, fill, then fall. At least she was warm to the touch. Decidedly warm, in fact. He put his hand on her forehead, scooping up the hair that lay over it. It was like a branding iron. He could hardly believe a human head could get so hot. He pulled the blanket down to her waist. She must have been running a fever. He didn't know what to do: get some water inside her, some aspirin, dampen her face? Perhaps it was best to let her sleep. Yet he couldn't quite convince himself that those dramatic flinches, her excessive temperature, weren't just strange symptoms of sleep that would vanish upon waking.

He knelt over her and kissed her ear. The cavity was hot. She stirred again. One arm stiffened, she seemed about to stretch, but all that happened was her body gave another jolt, and a stream of vomit jumped out of her mouth. It formed a yellow pool on the sand in front of her face, then soon drained away, leaving a residue of flecks on wet sand.

At that moment the door opened. It was a small, low board of battered wood studded with bolt-heads, which might once have been part of a grander door, and whistled over the sand. A man in sky-blue robes stooped into the room. He put a hand against his chest and coughed resonantly, then stood to his full height, a tall man, and said: '*Salaam aleikum.*' He dropped to the floor with his legs crossed.

Mortimer returned the greeting, then gestured at Celeste. '*Pas bon. Mal,*' he said. He pointed out the vomit on the floor, and added: '*Excusez-moi*,' then wiped her mouth with his sleeve, and went to his bag in search of something with which to mop the floor.

The man came forward and without hesitation scooped up the wet sand in his palm and left the room.

A water jar stood bedded into the sand in one corner. Mortimer had yet to drink from it. A moment ago he had lifted the lid, seen the glistening surface within, and postponed deciding if it was safe to drink. Now the only thing that mattered was to get some of it inside Celeste. But it wasn't easy. The jar was too heavy to lift, so he had to tip it over, which its round shape ought to have made easy, except that its bed in the sand held it firm. He had to use both hands. Which meant gauging where to put the cup on the floor, and he gauged wrong twice. Finally, he knelt beside Celeste with the cup half filled and attempted to raise her by the shoulders. She was heavy as a corpse, still fast asleep. Another tremor shook her. He put down the cup and brushed the hair off her cheek, wet with sweat. She twisted away and kicked, as a hoarse rattle escaped her, along with a thread of silver mucus.

Mortimer wiped it away. 'It's OK, it's OK.' He held the water to her lips, and it spilled over her chin. He couldn't tell if she swallowed any.

He had the idea of feeding her a pill. He had two he thought might be relevant: aspirin and Diocalm Plus. He didn't know if she had diarrhoea, but the pack claimed it would settle an upset stomach. Hence the 'Plus', he supposed.

He succeeded in getting her to swallow the two pills.

Not a minute later she vomited again, a gush of clear water that darkened the sand in front of her face. On it lay the two pills, completely intact.

The tall man returned, followed by a woman bundled up in robes and veil. Only by her shiny, wrinkled hands could Mortimer tell she was an elderly woman. It occurred to him that hands played a large part in local dancing because they were the one visible part of a woman's body.

'Do you speak French?' he tried.

The man glanced at him but said nothing. The woman took no notice at all, bowing over Celeste. Then she disappeared, returning soon with a second woman. Together the two of them lifted Celeste into a sitting position, talking to her quietly. Her head lolled on to her chest. They struggled to get her to her feet. The blankets slipped off, revealing bloodstains on her trousers. Mortimer's heart jumped in alarm. When he remembered that it was her period he was dismayed for her. The women put Celeste's arms round their necks and stood up. She let out a long, low sob, almost a bellow, and they shuffled out of the room with her between them.

The situation was hopeless until Mortimer found someone who could speak a word of French.

The tall man disappeared again, but soon came back, this time with two other men in tow. They all put their hands against their chests, then offered them to Mortimer. He shook, and one by one they patted their chests again. '*Bismillah*,' they said, dropping to the floor. Mortimer did the same. A boy came in and set a basket of dates on the floor. Mortimer didn't feel hungry, but once he bit into the sweet pulp he realised with a flush that he was starving. A clay jug arrived, and a metal beaker, and they passed around what he guessed must be sheep's milk, each taking a few sips of the thick, sweet liquid with its faintly rancid smell. Then in came a wooden bowl of couscous, and a pan of red sauce which one of the men tipped over the cereal. He fished out four spoons from somewhere in his robe and jammed them handle down in the sand. '*Bismillah*,' the men declared resonantly once more, and reached for the spoons.

Mortimer soon got the hang of the procedure, which was to excavate one's own eating cavity in the couscous against the nearest side of the bowl. When these pits were well established, another basket was brought in containing a plump organ, complete with the stumps of its severed arteries. One of the men growled approval, another grinned absent-mindedly, chewing as he watched the third tear the organ apart with his fingers and drop pieces of it in each eating hole.

Am I hungry enough to enjoy even this offal? wondered Mortimer. He probably had no choice anyway, if he wanted to keep on the right side of his hosts, and bit into the first chunk of the innard enthusiastically. But he wasn't hungry enough: it tasted of cement, of putrefaction, of dung, just like the dry, tough liver he had been forced to swallow at school. Sweat broke out on his brow and his gorge pumped. He fought it down, and meanwhile the man put another morsel in his crater. Mortimer smiled and nodded. The man looked back questioningly. '*Shokran*,' Mortimer added: Thank you.

The second piece he chewed hurriedly with head

bowed, packing in couscous around it. The third he swallowed without chewing at all, pretended to chew once it had gone down.

The distributor of the food watched him. He had brown eyes, not the usual black, and a short grey beard, revealed when he first rolled down his headscarf to eat.

The meal ended with rumbling belches, each one concluded with, '*Alhamdulillah*.' The brown-eyed man managed to get his belch to coincide with the uttering of thanks to God, so the word came out with a long, emphatic third syllable. How did they all have such deep voices? Perhaps some deformity of cosseted modern man squeezed his voice into his throat, where it didn't belong, whereas these laconic self-paced desert men spoke from the pit of the belly.

The men entered a discussion in the course of which a teapot emerged from the same man's robe who had had the spoons, along with two small tins. A charcoal brazier and four shot glasses arrived with the boy who came to clear away the meal.

Mortimer couldn't remember ever feeling so helpless. What was he supposed to do? He had never been anywhere where neither his French, Spanish nor English served him. And meanwhile Celeste was in the grip of fever and he couldn't even ask what they were doing with her. Perhaps they'd have traditional remedies, would know how to nurse her back to health with desert roots and minerals; presumably there weren't too many herbs out here. But where had they taken her? Did they know what was wrong with her?

And on top of all that, this wasn't news he was engaged in, but travel, the sort of thing that led to solemn literature about ennui in the desert. It irked him. In fact it panicked him. How was he going to get back to his job, get off this red herring? The last phrase made him think of his battered feet, and his mood plunged further. And he needed to pee, and even that he couldn't see how to communicate. Eventually he stood and stepped towards the door, which he now found was so low he would have to stoop to get out. He almost yelped with pain at the first few steps, and hobbled along, putting his weight on the sides of his feet.

All the men sprang up. They were less tall than he'd reckoned. He found his heart racing, and his face hot.

'*Excusez-moi. Toilette,*' he said.

They stared at him, their eyes bright, not happy. '*Toilette,*' he repeated. '*Salle de bain.*'

The bearded man with the brown eyes grunted something, and the smallest of them, a man with bulging eyes and a stubbled jaw, came forward to open the door. He led Mortimer down a passage so dark Mortimer could make out nothing except a fringe of rusty light at the far end. But the floor was sand and he trusted that there would be no obstacles. He stumbled along with one hand on the earth wall beside him, endeavouring to walk on the sides of his feet. The soles crunched with every step, burning and sparking. But that was better than setting them directly on the ground. The man turned down a staircase in pitch blackness, then along a short corridor, and finally down more stairs into an alley with daylight framed in a doorway at the end. The place was a regular labyrinth. As soon as Mortimer saw the daylight his feet began to hurt viciously. He limped along, and stopped to catch his breath.

They emerged into the splintered shade of a palm garden. The light was ferocious, even under the trees. Mortimer glanced up at the wall of the edifice from which he had emerged: fifty feet of solid mud. Last night, in the murky moments of their arrival, he had not taken it in. But the building was a single block of mud, with the warren of stairs and chambers burrowed out inside it. It was a massive defence against the sun.

The man led him along a raised path between two dry reservoirs, their caked beds stained white, and through a patch of small plants like young lettuces. Mortimer screwed up his eyes at the pain of his soles, and followed as fast as he could, each step seeming to blaze through his whole body. Finally, the man waved Mortimer towards a broken-down wall that might have been a ruined house. Beyond it rose a slope of sand flecked with dirt and stones. It was evidently the village refuse heap and lavatory, though it didn't smell bad.

Mortimer's urine sounded disconcertingly loud as it frothed on the sand.

On the walk back he saw camels grazing among the palms. He could hear their groaning and rumbling, as of rusty machines; the sound of camels at rest. A saddlepack sat on the ground under a tree with a water jar beside it. If they ever got out of here, that would be the way, he thought, what with his feet and Celeste's health. The prospect reassured him. If camels came, they could also leave.

Back in the room two new men had joined the others. These two were different, wore copious black headpieces shaped like drums, like Orthodox mitres. They held black veils over their faces with fine fingers, and glanced at Mortimer with flashing eyes. Two Tuareg. He had never actually set eyes on one close up before. They didn't return his greeting. None of the men did. Something wasn't right. Mortimer felt his chest constrict. The two visitors had muskets resting across their laps. There was no other word for their antiquated broad-barrelled weaponry, which most likely had been brought along as part of a man's formal attire, Mortimer guessed, rather than for imminent use. But they were still alarming to see in this small, earthen shelter. Alarming, then somehow satisfying.

No war without its correspondent, the thought came to Mortimer. Wars that had no reporter had no existence. There had never been a war without its chronicler, from Homer onwards.

Still no one greeted him. The man who had conducted him to the midden sat down again, so Mortimer did the same, with his back to the door but near it, slightly apart from the loose circle the men made, as if he didn't want to presume or intrude, but equally didn't want to appear aloof, still less timid. Something made this a delicate situation, he could sense it.

No one said anything for what seemed an interminable time. Then the door scraped open and another local came in, followed by three more Tuareg. It seemed that only Mortimer turned to look and nod. The newcomers sat down. More silence. At first Mortimer took it to be an uncomfortable silence, until it occurred to him that perhaps the men might be happy to sit quietly. Probably for visitors and hosts alike, this was an unusually busy day as it was. In the desert one could go years without visitors. Mortimer began to feel comfortable too, and realised that he too could sit waiting without a thought in his mind. In his own small way he too had had his baptism in the desert, he knew something of the danger of being out on the sand, and of the inner calm surviving it instilled.

His and Celeste's bags stood in a far corner of the room. He began to wish they were elsewhere. They seemed a graphic representation of his intrusion.

The door opened again, allowing in another local man dressed in sky-blue robes. He came in talking to himself, and unwrapped his scarf to reveal a scalp of silver stubble, a sunburnt glistening face and fleshy protuberant lips. It was a moment before Mortimer realised the man was speaking a heavily accented French directed at him. He was saying, '*Vite, vite*, I came quick as I could, as soon as they found me. The monsieur speaks no Saharawi, they said, so it is my pleasure to speak French. We must leave these gentlemen, we will leave now. *Venez vite, monsieur.*'

None of the others made any sign of having noticed the new arrival.

'These are the bags?' the man went on, crossing over to them. He had spectacular buck teeth, such that he couldn't close his lips.

A husky, deep voice said something, and the man stopped.

'*Venez, monsieur,*' he repeated, returning to the door without the bags, and sending Mortimer a toothy grin.

Mortimer said, 'Will you please tell these men that I am honoured to be in their presence, and thank them for their hospitality?'

No reply came to the translated message, except for one deep belch. For a moment Mortimer was torn: whether to push it, to attempt right now, from the start, to be present; or to leave. He quickly concluded the moment was too sensitive, and he must go. He wouldn't be going far anyway, with Celeste in the state she was in. He pulled on his boots as gently as he could, laced them halfway, and let the heels drag as they left the room. The small man reached back to pull the door to. Mortimer heard an utterance beyond it, and a reply. The talk beginning? Had they been waiting for him to leave?

'*Les bagages?*' he asked as they filed down the passage.

'Later,' the man said.

Mortimer's feet were burning. For a moment the pain seemed so livid and intense he felt he had no choice but to give in to it entirely. His eyes moistened in the dark. He blinked and tried to steady his breath.

They had to press against the rough wall to allow a pair of boys to pass, who went scurrying on leaving an aroma of rosewater behind them.

'*Et ma femme?*' Mortimer asked.

The man glanced at him. Mortimer could just make out his eyes gleaming in the dark. '*Oui, oui,*' he said.

Outside, the man paused to introduce himself as

Hamed, shaking Mortimer's hand and giving him another display of his teeth. Mortimer had not noticed that Hamed had a bayonet thrust in his belt. He led Mortimer along the wall of the ksar, this time the other way. Mortimer traipsed along behind him, every step a step of fire. He wanted to weep: what a helpless state he was in; he couldn't speak to anyone, and he couldn't even walk.

Then they turned the corner, and a host of camels came into view, some seated on the ground under the palms with their front feet tucked neatly under their chests like cats, others standing on open ground beyond, ropes hanging from their chins. The impression was of light but immensely tall beasts. A few men robed in black stood among the camels, others sat in small groups, here and there a wisp of smoke rose.

A spurt of delirious excitement ran through him. Here he was, just what they needed, right in their midst. They didn't yet know their incredible good fortune, and he was just discovering his. *No war without its chronicler.* They shared in the same stroke of brilliant luck, he and they. He had judged right in giving himself to chance, and now it would – it could – pay off spectacularly for all of them. If only they could be made to realise it. The question of the bags and their contents – press cards, notebooks, cameras – had been troubling him, but now he knew beyond doubt that he had no choice but to be open with these people. They would surely go through the bags. He wanted them to know as soon as possible that he was here, the man who could champion them, raise their cause from obscurity.

Then a horrible misgiving hit. Suppose they simply rejected the edict of fate, and sent him on his way?

'*Ma femme,*' he said again. 'Where is she?'

Hamed was leading him down a long path under palms. Mortimer could see no house ahead, but he couldn't imagine they would have taken Celeste far.

And it would be a great stroke of luck for her too, once she was better. She was in the midst of a treasure trove of classic shots. If this story turned out the way it might, and if the two of them did everything they might with it, they could become an impregnable team.

'*Oui, oui,*' Hamed repeated, as if he knew all about Celeste's whereabouts. Mortimer felt a twinge of doubt that he might know nothing at all, hadn't even understood his question.

'*Et Brahim?*' Mortimer tried as he hobbled along. The question had been bothering him.

'Brahim?' Hamed asked.

'The man with the donkey.' He waited a moment to see if that would help. 'The man who brought us here.'

Hamed shrugged. 'He has gone.'

Mortimer asked, 'Where?' as if it could possibly matter. Perhaps he hoped to find out if there was still the shadow of a possibility of leaving the way they had come. He felt alarmed that Brahim could have left without them.

'*Il est parti,*' Hamed said again. 'He has a long way to go.'

The desert was a mystery: an empty land in which people appeared beside one along the way, then vanished. One had to pursue one's own business. But he wished he had a proper contact. He was so unprepared. It was exasperating. If he could only find one person in the leadership – assuming they had one – who had had some broader experience, who had been to Algiers, knew a minister, a colonel, who had heard of *Le Monde*, who knew there was a world churning and clanging along beyond the desert. Whether or not this person might care for that world was another matter, but perhaps if he didn't Mortimer could persuade him to, at least enough to let that world know what was going on down here. Assuming that he himself could establish what was going on.

They passed into a straggle of old earth homes, ordinary desert houses that the man identified as the *vieux ksar*. By comparison, the main ksar seemed like a new apartment block to which the well-to-do had fled from this chain of ruinous slums. The furthest houses of the two rows were half buried in sand. Mortimer could see a set of palm fronds halfway up one dune, sprouted there with no trunk at all, like a plant strange to these parts. Another palm had a trunk only a few feet tall. One red wall ran straight into the sand. It was clear what was happening: the dunes were swamping these houses, and this would sooner or later be a sunken village.

Hamed stopped and opened a door. As soon as Mortimer entered, a woman left with a rustling of robes, so promptly he hardly got a look at her.

He saw Celeste lying on her side against a far wall on a kind of shelf, covered in a grey blanket. He knelt over her. Her throat rattled softly with each breath. Even in the gloom he could see her face was red with sunburn.

The room seemed cooler than in the other ksar, and there was something comforting about being in an ordinary dishevelled house. It seemed a better place for her to be. A transistor radio had been attached to a wall with wire, various plastic bags hung from nails, on a bench against the furthest darkest wall lay a heap of rumpled linen.

He put his hand under Celeste's blanket. She was hot like a furnace, and damp. Perhaps that was good, she was sweating out the fever. And she was still sleeping, which could only be a good thing.

Hamed left. Alone, Mortimer tried to gather his thoughts. But it was impossible that he sit tight here with Celeste as she slept while a troop of nomads with muskets held war councils not quarter of a mile away. On the other hand, it was exhilarating beyond measure to be in the right spot. Assuming, again, that the accounts were true that the Tuareg were none too happy about Algeria's plans for the Sahara, and that there was indeed a resistance brewing.

Mortimer put his head out the door. A quiet sunlit morning in a village. A cock crowed somewhere, a hen crooned, and he could hear a goat bleating. It was a scene of remote, immemorial peace.

Over the brow of a dune at the end of the row of houses a black shape appeared. The shape swayed, grew, rising from behind the sand, and became the top half of a man. He floated along the brow for a while, swaying backwards and forwards, then rose higher, and the head of a camel appeared, bobbing back and forth. The rest of the beast gradually rose from the sand. The man must have been sixty yards away. Up on the animal, he looked huge. He crossed the brow and began to descend the village side, towards the ksar. Already another rider was bobbing up from behind the dune, and behind him another. From the saddle of each of them a stick pointed diagonally to the sky. Mortimer stood watching as more and more riders glided out of the sand.

If Kepple could see me now, he thought, and grinned. Something was getting up, and no mistake. But who was paying for it?

Hamed came running down the track. '*Si, si*,' he called, grinning from exertion. He held a small brazier in one hand and a plastic bag in the other. '*Du thé*,' he said, holding up the tea things.

They sat on the floor of the house while Hamed brewed up. Celeste inhaled sharply once, and let out a long moan. Mortimer thought she was waking but she slept on. Is she going to get a surprise when she pulls through, he thought to himself.

12

It was not a good day. Mortimer tried to get out of the house numerous times, but Hamed was adamant that they stay where they were. Later on a boy arrived with Celeste's two bags, walking stiffly under their weight, and left without a word. Ten minutes later he came back with Mortimer's bag.

Women came and went. They would put their head in the door, say something to Hamed, and disappear again. Sometimes they studied Celeste, stroked her head, tucked her up, and left.

Later, Celeste rubbed her face, said, 'Strange sleep,' and began to sit up, then groaned and lay back down. Mortimer squeezed himself on to the bench beside her. She was hot still, but less so, more like the ordinary warmth of someone rousing from a long sleep. Hamed was sitting on the ground outside at the time.

'I was worried about you,' Mortimer said, stroking her hair.

She shuddered, turned to the wall and was sick again. He fished a dirty shirt out of his bag and wiped away the dribble she had produced. She sat with her hands round her knees, and shivered. 'I'm so cold.'

He laid her back down and covered her with the blanket, then pulled out his jacket and draped it over her. He unfolded a sheet off the pile against the far wall and laid that on her too. In spite of all this, and even though it was warm and stuffy in the room, her teeth chattered. He lay down beside her, felt her jolt in his arms and her jaw shudder as he held her. Eventually she became still.

Hamed said, '*C'est le soleil.*' But it seemed impossible that the sun alone could do this.

Hamed came by later with an old-looking rectangular battery with long brass electrodes, a kind of battery

Mortimer had used in his bicycle headlamp as a boy. Hamed hooked it up to wires dangling from the base of the radio on the wall, flicked a switch, leaving the battery hanging there, and produced a whistle and crackle of static. He commenced searching for a station. A raucous Arabic voice with jangling music in the background shouted for a moment. Then a woman's voice, so fuzzed by static even Hamed could probably not understand it. Finally he hit on a military band playing a sprightly march, and stopped there. In a moment an old-fashioned English voice, the voice of another era, was declaring that this was the World Service.

It was extraordinary to hear, not so much because of the impossibly remote and timeless setting in which Mortimer was listening to it, but because of the world from which the clipped male voice seemed to come: a world of old-fashioned pre-war cars and buses, of steamships and Morse code, a world of radar and propeller planes. What had happened while he had been gone?

In the afternoon he took an aspirin to ease the pain in his feet, and shuffled off to where the camels were resting under the palms. There must have been fifty or more, and as many riders. Here and there men had spread reed mats on the sand, and frayed strips of rug on which to perform their prayers.

'*Salaam aleikum,*' people called out, and invited him to join them. They'd roll down their headscarves from dark faces and sit up, accept a cigarette from him with lean, brown fingers that emerged from their copious robes, and Mortimer would settle on the ground.

Such calm men, he wrote in his notebook later. *They laze around the tea-fires all day, seemingly barely moving, yet you sense that at any moment they could spring into action. Both idle and alert: something we don't know how to do in the West. No one knows how to laze like desert men, with their fine fingers and smooth, dark faces, who do not stand when they can sit, or sit when they can lie. Yet they are decorous and considerate, the last bearers of some lost civilisation where people were more stately, gracious.*

I get offered tea everywhere, and must always stay for three glasses. Out come the tiny blue pot, the plastic bags of mint and sugar, of fierce grey 'chinois noir'. Then the shot glasses twisted into the sand. No warming the pot. They just pour in the water, add a palmful of tea, and set the whole lot on the fire. When it begins to fizz they drop in a great lump of sugar and the interminable frothing begins: pot to glass and glass to pot, back and forth in the highest arc you can manage. The idea is to get up a good sweet froth. But the first glass is never sweet. The tea is too bitter. You can hardly get it down, it's so strong. Bitter like life, they say. They always have three rounds. The second is better: they add the mint, and more sugar. Strong like love. The third is easiest of all. Sweet like death. A sentiment peculiar to the desert?

I've never seen anything like the flies here. The tea-pouring attracts them. They settle all over one's fingers. Once the glass is in your hand, they line the rim completely, like margarita salt. Try to wave them away and they ignore you. Only if you touch them will they reluctantly step on to their neighbour and angrily buzz away. You lift the glass to your lips. Inches from your mouth, there they are still. Just as you think: fuck it, I'm never going to be able to drink this. Or else: fuck it, I'm just going to have to swallow a couple of flies, they vanish. Lower the cup an inch and there they are again.

A funny thing: how I like it here. How it suits me.

About the guns. Men want clarity and simplicity and that is what guns offer. Guns make life simple. They feel right, they clarify life. They give you direction. They make a man feel loved.

The room, the little house, began to feel wonderful once the afternoon drew into evening. Mortimer sensed that the crisis was past, and there was nowhere like a sick-room when the worst was over. It stirred memories of the comfort of being tended in his room when sick as a child, at an hour when he should have been at school.

Two women arrived with a clay bowl of water. Hamed and Mortimer left the room. Outside the sky was luminous, a sheet of electric lilac. Against it, the walls of the houses were dark, and glimmered like velvet. Palm fronds glistened, stirred by a light breeze. A gentle roar reached Mortimer's ears from somewhere in the distance, like a fleet of motors idling. It was the camels. Then a voice rang out, calling men to prayer, rising like a siren, holding a long note that mutated, moving through different vowels, and falling away. It rose and fell again, the herald of night.

Hamed fetched a kerosene lamp, dazzling to look at, yet casting a weak watery light around the room. The rafters, the walls, all were plunged into blackness, as if the little hissing light merely threw objects back into greater darkness.

The worst was not over. Celeste was feverish most of the night. Her teeth started chattering again, her lips vibrated as she inhaled, stuttering as if she was on the point of a seizure. A white line of spume formed on her lip. 'So cold,' she muttered, shivering. Mortimer piled all his clothes on her, then wrapped another sheet over them, making a great bundle out of her bed. He lay on the floor beside her.

He was woken by a cry in the middle of the night, and found himself lying under a heap of his own clothes. Celeste was on the bench above, writhing and groaning. He tried to get her to drink some water, wiped back the hair stuck to her cheek, but she recoiled at his touch. '*Non, non, non.*'

He felt useless, hopelessly ill-equipped to nurse her.

At one point Mortimer crept past Hamed, who was slumped against the wall by the door, and went out into a night lit by a high quarter-moon. By the time he got to the end of the row of houses and caught a glimpse of the field of black shapes camped out under the stars, someone was at his elbow. It gave him a shock. He hadn't heard Hamed following.

He must learn to wait, that was all. That would be the desert's first lesson: patience. In such a beautiful scene – the silky land shimmering under the moon, the palms glazed and motionless, and all the desert men dozing by their beasts – it was easy to be a willing pupil.

13

He woke to find Hamed shaking him by the arm. A tall Tuareg made taller still by his headpiece was standing in the room. He loomed as a single piece of perfect blackness in the dark. Mortimer glanced at his watch: three thirty in the morning. '*Bon soir,*' he said, and stood up.

The Tuareg put a hand to his own chest.

Hamed knelt to pump the kerosene lamp. It took a lot of pumping, and fiddling with the valves, but eventually spurted into flame, settling into a loud hiss as the bulb sparked and incandesced.

'*Monsieur Mortimer, vous êtes bienvenues,*' the tall Tuareg said in perfect French, in what seemed the deepest voice Mortimer had yet heard.

At last, Mortimer thought: the interpreter he had been waiting for. He went to his bag and rummaged through a side pocket. Hamed appeared at his elbow, watching. Mortimer frowned at him. When he turned back into the room with his press card, the Tuareg had stepped back and was watching intently.

Mortimer held out the card. 'I'm a journalist, from the *Tribune.*'

'We know who you are,' the man said in his good French, gesturing that they should seat themselves on the floor. 'What we do not know is how you come to be here.'

Mortimer was about to answer: by pure chance, *par hazard*, but he felt it to be an inadequate explanation.

'I was coming down to report on the Sahelian drought,' he said. 'Then I heard about things going on with the Tuareg, and we happened to be passing through Timimoun.'

'Things going on with the Tuareg? What had you heard?'

'That the Tuareg were unhappy with the president's Saharan initiative.'

'The government can do what they like, as long as they leave us alone. But who suggested you come here?'

'My editor at the *Tribune*.'

'We must have a name.'

'He's called Kepple.'

The Tuareg shook his head.

'Is the *Tribune* not enough of a name?'

He shook his head again. 'Not enough.'

The lamp hissed. They sat for a moment saying nothing. Mortimer waited, and realised that the man would wait too. It was up to him, Mortimer, to make a move. He would have to do it. He shrugged. 'I have a friend in Algiers.'

The inevitable question came: 'Who?'

There was nothing for it, he would have to use Taillot's name, and just hope that it would do no harm. It was appalling to be so hopelessly unvouched-for.

He mentioned Taillot, realising as he did so that he didn't even know his first name, let alone what he really did, or who he was. He was just one of Kepple's tricks, conjured from the *demi-monde* of international advisers and observers. But he was evidently something in Algiers, and Mortimer had a hunch that he just might be known of down here. Why else would he first have suggested Mortimer come, then tried to scare him off?

In the fierce light of the kerosene stove the man's eyes shone hazel, translucent. He said nothing, but pulled down his shesh, revealing a smooth face coloured an even nut brown. There was a mournful slant to his eyes, and his eyebrows rose a little in the middle, above the bridge of his nose. He looked slightly sad, and friendly. There were dimples round his mouth. His age was hard to judge but surely not less than forty. He was clean-shaven, but Mortimer guessed he was a man who would not have to shave often.

He said something to Hamed in Arabic. Hamed left.

The visitor treated the late-night hour like any other. One was awake: what did the hour matter? He showed no sign of fatigue at all, other than the general weightiness of his bearing. The thought crossed Mortimer's mind: this was a man on the eve of battle.

'And Rio Camello?' the Tuareg asked.

Mortimer shrugged and looked away.

'You were down there, no?'

Mortimer racked his brains for how the man could possibly know. There were only two ways: either he did know Taillot, and Taillot had told him; or else he read the newspapers and had seen Mortimer's reports from the Rio Camello territory. He nodded. 'A few weeks ago, yes.'

'So now you have a chance to see things from the other side,' the Tuareg said.

It was a comment that puzzled Mortimer. Surely the Rio Camello could in no way be construed as the Tuareg's foe. He asked: '*Vous êtes Marocain?*'

The man tutted and shook his head. '*Je suis Tuareg.*'

Perhaps he simply meant that the Tuareg were struggling against the state that supported Rio Camello, namely Algeria.

The man asked: 'Do you think you know why we are here?'

Mortimer demurred with something general. 'For a long time the Tuareg have wanted their autonomy.'

'For a long time the Tuareg have had their autonomy. Even the French never brought us under their law. We have our own law. We are like a river: anyone who tries to stop us, we flow another way. We are the only people to whom the desert is a true home.' He gestured around the room. 'That is why we have no need of houses. For us, a house is a tomb. We live on the sand, under the stars. We have always lived this way, we are the oldest people on earth, our ancestry reaches back to before the Flood. We alone of men never stooped to sow seeds. Our problem is just beginning with this government. They want to build a road to Niger, no problem. We simply walk our camels across the highway when we need to. They build some more houses in Tamanrasset or In Salah, no problem. Our problem is the oil. This is our land. We want nothing from anybody, only to be left alone, not to be like your Indians in America, shipped off our native land and moved where you will. We will never allow that. But in order to protect ourselves we need money. That is the only persuasion those people understand. Why should they suck the money out of our ancestral land? Why should we allow them to let the Americans suck it away? Once they come in, everything will change. We are not fools, we know what has happened in other places, in Arabia and the Emirates. Where are the Bedou's tents now?'

The man hummed, then went on: 'We have friends. We have people who will help us. But we need more. We can do much with a camel and a rifle, but it is doubtful we can do enough. If Monsieur Taillot directed you here he would have a reason, *n'est-ce-pas?*'

Mortimer ran his fingers over the sand between his knees. 'If you think I can help,' he said. All the more fortunate, he thought, that he had not heeded Taillot's warning to stay away.

The man glanced at the sleeping form on the bunk. 'And her?'

'She is a photographer. Celeste Dumas.'

'It is a difficult situation. We are not alone.'

'Shall we go outside?' Mortimer asked.

But apparently that wasn't what he meant. He tutted, then got up, bowed, gave his name as Jean Baptiste, and left.

Hamed came back inside. He and Mortimer sat in silence listening to the rustle of the kerosene lamp. After a while Mortimer lay down. He didn't sleep. As he lay on the earth floor he saw himself as a tiny figure pinned to the great flat world. He could feel gravity holding him down, his limbs splayed against the ground. The flat plate of the world slowly turned, carrying him with it. In a while he would be no more. Before then all he could do was scurry about with great industry, caught in a frantic round of activity, achieving nothing, or at best very little. But he didn't mind. It felt like a glorious privilege.

The lamp hissed. The walls were black. A lone cicada chirruped. Meanwhile, outside, the sleeping nomads floated on the earth beside their resting barks.

Mortimer reflected that Jean Baptiste had given his name only at the very end, as if he'd been reluctant to do so earlier. He wondered about that. Was there some kind of Tuareg belief, analogous to the Amerindian taste for silence before commencing a conversation, or the primitive fear of a camera, that held a name a talisman? Either way it seemed promising that Jean Baptiste had shared his name, and had already known Mortimer's. Perhaps that would give the Tuareg a reassuring sense of having a hold over him; if a few hundred guns didn't do that already.

Jean Baptiste returned in a while. He evidently had no plans for sleeping that night. He offered the chest-patting greeting perfunctorily, as if the gesture were merely a salute, and announced, slightly out of breath, that an important person was on his way.

Mortimer scrambled to his feet, which blazed with pain once more. He bent double, groaning, and slumped to the ground apologising, then pulled on his boots carefully. He really had to do something about his feet. Jean Baptiste merely looked at him and told him to cover the woman's head.

Two local men appeared in the doorway, whispering, '*Bismillah*.' They stepped inside with heads bowed. After them came an old man dressed in white robes and carrying a stick. He too uttered the name of God, in a reedy, piercing tenor.

Mortimer at once felt uneasy. The old man had a thin mouth, the top lip drawn up, revealing yellow stumps of teeth, and his eyes were puffy and bloodshot, full of mistrust. He stared at Mortimer with a sneer. Mortimer would have to tread carefully. He almost felt betrayed by this old man already: he could sense that the man had the power to block him from the role he was meant to play. It was unfair. Bitter old men should not have the right to come between a man and his work. He could feel the man's sneer as a sensation in his own belly, a twist of scorn.

The man gave a sermon, interpreted by Jean Baptiste. Did Mortimer realise a man could be pulverised into a thousand thousand pieces – Jean Baptiste made a point of repeating the number, as the old man presumably did somewhere in the thick of his Koranic invective – and every single one of those pieces would spend a thousand eternities in each of thirty-three hells, if he so much as thought of impeding a jihad? Mortimer did not have to answer the question, because the man's voice kept rolling on in its reedy twang, his lips turned out as if the words were sour in his mouth. He clutched his stick tightly, sometimes tapping it on the sand, sometimes jabbing it in Mortimer's direction. Throughout the oration he stared at a point on the wall to Mortimer's left. Eventually he fell silent, and settled his gaze on Mortimer's face. Mortimer bowed his head in what he imagined to be an attitude of reverence. He wasn't sure if a reply was expected, or if the man were merely probing his soul with those merciless eyes. Mortimer hedged his bets and said, '*Merci.*'

One of the men accompanying the holy man was chubby, with a long Pancho Vila moustache. He sat motionless, fat fingers entwined, elbows on knees. It was he who broke the silence, in a rough, guttural French. 'You see that stick he is holding.' He pointed at the mullah's staff. His eyes slid over Mortimer in a way he could physically sense in his skin. 'If he wanted to, he could point that stick at you and you would no longer be there.' The man stared at Mortimer to see that the point had been made. 'Or he could throw it on the ground at your feet and it would become a serpent and bite you.'

A magic wand, Mortimer thought. He bowed again solemnly. His heart was thumping.

The old man began a high, insistent chant which suited his reedy voice. He had the voice of a shawm, full of dextrous inflection. The others joined in, in thick basses. They stared at Mortimer as they held their notes, their necks twitching and pulsing. Then Jean Baptiste sang too, in a softer voice, humming along compliantly. Mortimer wondered, under all their gazes, if he was expected to join in.

The old man's vocal line became higher and more intricate, an exotic descant borne along above the obbligato of bass, which then ceased, leaving his line high up on its own, his tune fluttering, dipping and swooping like a bird. It was something of a feat, and Mortimer assumed they were all to pay it special attention. But the man with the Mexican moustache addressed Mortimer right across it, with the half-pious, half-authoritarian smile of a pastor before a roomful of Sunday school kids. 'You must say this,' he said, and launched into a prayer.

Mortimer had no choice, he repeated each line as requested. '*Lah ilaha ulallah.*' Meanwhile, the high voice buzzed and fluted on its own ecstatic trajectory.

Perhaps they felt it wouldn't matter much either way. Perhaps they reflected that Allah had seen fit to set Mortimer among them. Perhaps he was now one of the saved, having pronounced the necessary formulas. Either way, he was on board. They took him along.

14

The day began with a long camel ride.

As soon as the mullah finished his ceremonials a boy entered the room with a plastic bowl and a brass jug. He went round the men in turn, pouring out a stream of rose-scented water in which they washed their hands. The mullah's lustrations extended to his feet too. After pouring, the youth would flip a thin towel off his shoulder.

Outside, there was no shouting of commands, no apparent staff. Camels were brought to their knees, groaning and grunting, while others were levering themselves to their full height with the dark bundle of a rider on their backs, and some were already walking through the dark, as if they were the true leaders and instigators.

Jean Baptiste got Mortimer on his mount. For a moment he seemed inexperienced with the animal. When he tugged on its halter to get it to kneel, he succeeded only in making it circle round them. He swore quietly, clucked at it, held his stick to its neck. With great reluctance, with a shuffling of its hoofs and lifting of the high neck, and a whinnying grunt, the animal dropped laboriously to its knees.

The saddle consisted of a lot of blankets, with somewhere among them a layer of sheepskin showing a woolly edge. There was a wooden pommel, which Mortimer gripped before straddling the animal horseback-style. Jean Baptiste made him dismount and reboard side-saddle, with the pommel tucked into the crook of a knee. It seemed a precarious position, but like jump-starting a motorbike it was easier to balance than it looked.

Far ahead Mortimer could see riders filing up a dune, a procession of dark shapes flowing up the pallor beyond the palms. He had not ridden a camel before, and was alarmed at first by the height, then exhilarated, seeming to soar through the high air of dawn. But he hated to leave Celeste behind, and in the state she was in. He didn't know what else to do, though. They had given him no time. And he had no choice, he had to go with them.

There was a faint smell of sour milk about his animal. He passed other riders who had not yet mounted, one or two even still lying on the ground, their mounts resting like boulders beside them. He was relieved not to have to tell his animal where to go, or give it any kind of instruction. It knew where to go, caught in the general flow, which seemed no single person's decision. Riders streamed out of the palms like a fleet of boats on a current. To Mortimer, riding high on a level with all the others, it was as if the beasts had coalesced into a single transport for the field.

Already the sky was fading from its intense black. A last star burned ahead.

As if to underline the singularity of the body of motion, the sound of the camels' hoofs was a single hiss, like the sound of skis in snow. Mortimer listened, and could not distinguish the footfalls of his own mount from the general sibilance. Behind, he could hear a series of grunts emanating from some obstreperous beast, then a tremendous bellowing, which sustained itself a moment and died away. Someone was clicking his tongue. Someone else exhorted his ride in a rhythmic incantation: *ha-ta, ha-ta, ha-ta.* Beneath all these sounds, the single susurrus of the camels' feet continued. A moment later another rider pronounced the same exhortation closer by. *Ha-ta!*

No man could resist the allure of publicity, Mortimer reflected. It amplified and liberated a cause to know that it was going to be written about, would achieve fame. Fame, and through that a chance at immortality: it elevated what was a skirmish, a brawl, a half-baked and shoddy-looking enterprise, into a moment of history with a place in the annals.

He was sure he could detect a change in the rebels. They seemed to have not so much renewed conviction as liberation from conviction: as if it was no longer necessary to convince themselves of their cause, now that the action would be launched on a broader stage, would be widely known. It was as if the training wheels had been taken off a bicycle.

This was how it struck Mortimer as they rode through the chalky dawn. It could have been, though, that the sense of a new and higher motivation in the men derived from their having at last commenced an operation. Their gathering had been given the momentum it wanted.

A series of light thumpings became audible: someone moving up from behind in a canter. The muffled drumming of the hoofs became insistent to Mortimer's ear, growing louder. Then it ceased, receded into the general sound, and Jean Baptiste was at Mortimer's side, rocking gently.

Mortimer didn't recognise him at first, with only his eyes showing through his scarf. He unwrapped the cloth and handed it to Mortimer, mimed wrapping it round his own head, by which Mortimer understood that he was to wear it himself. He smiled at the way the two of them could have conversed had they wanted to, rocking along at the same height, ignoring their mounts, like two people in a chairlift. Jean Baptiste seemed to have nothing in particular to say, he merely wanted Mortimer to wear the shesh. He fell in as an escort, something Mortimer was happy to have.

Getting the shesh in place was a two-handed operation, and meant letting go of the saddle's pommel. The cloth was long, ten feet or more, and he had to wrap it round numerous times before he felt enough was enough and tucked a copious tail end in one of the folds. He felt hot and slightly sick. The cloth smelled of fresh paint. Was it really necessary to add to one's clothing like this? The sun wasn't even up.

But it soon would be. The world was light now. They rose over a shoulder of sand and down into a long defile of gravel, and what looked like shattered concrete.

Mortimer wondered if it was the same gully that Brahim had brought them down on their way into the village. After a while he saw a great buttress of red cliff ahead, and recognised the ruined fort clinging to the spine of the ridge. That was where the sun first struck: a filament of bright yellow showed at the top. It was a marvellous sight: the body of smoky crimson rock edged by a fine line, a crust of light, like a skin on cream, or a hunk of cheese with that hard bright rind to it.

Jean Baptiste reached out to Mortimer with a handful of sticky crystallised date pulp, a staple of the desert. It could last for years before going stale, he had heard. Several times he was given a tin cup of water as he rode, never enough. He'd down it before he knew what he had done, and be surprised at the sight of the yellowed bottom with no more in it. At one point he found himself horribly bored, bobbing along like this up and down shallow dunes of yellow sand that stretched on for ever. The dunes here seemed paler than the deep orange-gold of three days before. Then he'd remember what was going on – the posse of riders about him, the warmongering caravan spiked with gun barrels – and feel acutely fearful. What had he got himself into? This wasn't his war. He had no war. What an idiotic thing it would be to get killed, or even hurt. He seriously considered turning back. But would he find his way? The desert killed you if you got lost. And would they let him go anyway? Now as he thought back he realised he had never actually stated that he wished to ride with them. Perhaps they thought the boot was on the other foot, and they were taking him with them whether he wanted to come or not. And anyway, how on earth would he broach the subject of turning back? It was unthinkable. The march was on, it was happening, and he was part of it.

But it would make one hell of a story. He could already imagine himself seizing a hotel telephone to call through his copy. Of course, he'd have to have written something first.

Then a different fear would seize him: what if all this led to nothing, to an insignificant skirmish, a quick pacifying gesture by the authorities to keep the rebels happy? And they'd all go back to their flocks and Mortimer would have a travel piece on his hands.

Were they perhaps heading for Timimoun? he wondered. He thought they might be travelling east, in the town's direction, but the sun was already too high for him to be sure. And now that he thought about it he wasn't sure that Timimoun was to the east anyway. If only one could get hold of a decent map. He had a vague idea that a road continued south-west beyond Timimoun, but he couldn't think why any route would do that. He had no recollection of there being any settlement in that direction before the Western Sahara and Mauritania.

Flies had settled on his hands. He gave up trying to send them away. Whatever he did, they only came back. They seemed to favour the cuticles. Several jostled one another in a line across his fingers. Knuckle dusters, he thought, and waved his hand in the air. They clung on doggedly, he really had to shake to get them off, and they immediately came back when he stopped.

Then another fear arose, a cloying anxiety about Celeste. Something might happen to her while he was gone; she might be alarmed to find herself alone; she might even recover and up sticks, slip out of his life before he could get back, believing that was what he had done. He couldn't bear the thought of her suffering in his absence, of not being there to comfort her. He might be the one living solace to her and he had abandoned her, sick, in an oasis a thousand miles from anywhere. What did it say about him that so carelessly, so blithely he could walk away from something he had never known before, an unassailable, unasked-for intimacy with another person? He knew the value of work but not love? Was he already becoming the kind of pseudo-tough guy who lied to himself that he didn't care about things he did? Journalism was full of men like that. You could recognise them before they even opened their mouths. They weren't any fun to look in the eye.

But Celeste would understand the need to get after the story. Even when they were delivered to you on a plate, stories still had to be followed through, constructed, given substance. He was determined to get himself into the foreign print game, to make it to the front, and rightly or wrongly he had put work first, and if he had done so without a second thought at least he was having second thoughts now. If it turned out to be a mistake, then that was the way life went – but a trapdoor gave way as he reached the end of that thought: if he lost her, he wouldn't forgive himself.

He couldn't keep himself from the thought that in

every life there came a turning point, one crucial moment when all that person's strength was summoned for a trial, not exactly between right and wrong, but between integrity and cowardice, gratitude and cynicism, courage and self-deceit. He couldn't just clop away from her over the dunes like this, without at least letting her know.

Just before leaving, he had knelt over her, meaning to shake her awake and tell her he was going. But she had been sleeping so deeply, the breaths rustling in and out of her divine, once-broken nose, her face calm, that he couldn't bring himself to. So he had written a brief note: *They're off, and they're taking me with them. I'm sorry*, he added. *You're sick, you must rest, forgive me. Will be back as soon as possible.* Then came the decision, which absurdly he found excruciating, how to sign off. *I love you?* He hadn't yet written that to her. Would it seem flippant, coming at the end of such a brief note, which for all he knew she might see as a professional betrayal? Then he had the idea: no note. The message of that would be: they have whisked me off. Just as he was deliberating, Jean Baptiste had swung open the door and said, '*On y va.*' Mortimer had crumpled the paper and stuffed it in his trouser pocket and slipped out into the night.

He had been feeling that ball of paper against his thigh as he rode. Now that they had been on the hoof three or four hours, his sweat and body-warmth, the kneading under the stretched cloth of his trousers as the camel walked, had softened the paper to the point where he could no longer feel it.

Mortimer looked round for Jean Baptiste, but he had moved off.

'*Ça va?*' asked a deep voice behind him. He twisted in his saddle. Sure enough Jean Baptiste was right there, just behind.

Mortimer's heart beat hard, and he felt the blood in his face as he said: 'I have been thinking. I must go back.'

Jean Baptiste made no response. Before he could, two camel riders who had found enough reserves of strength within their beasts to come trotting up through the field passed by, then pulled on their reins and slowed up ahead. One had to pull harder and longer than the other, and jogged about in the saddle as he did so, in a way that seemed less comfortable than the rest of the riders. The first rider spoke to Jean Baptiste and they both laughed. His face was covered with a scarf, as was Baptiste's, yet they both knew right away who the other was.

The second rider urged his camel on, holding the reins unusually high, slipping precariously in the saddle and failing to regain his seat as the animal skipped about, snorting. He attempted to steer it in front of Baptiste, then towards Mortimer, but only succeeded in cantering across the general flow of riders.

Mortimer caught up with the camel.

The rider turned round in the saddle and pulled away the scarf. It was Celeste. She wiped her red and glistening face. 'They didn't give me any choice. These two men just about dragged me from bed. *Le monsieur n'a pas la machine. Pas machine. Madame a la machine. Machine?* What are they on about? Then I got it. They shoved my camera bag round my neck and threw me on a camel. Here I am. At least the ride seems to have done me some good. I feel human again.'

'You're fantastic,' he called, and laughed, urging his camel closer. It seemed near-miraculous that she had come, and just when he had decided to go back to her.

'Thank God you're better. I was terrified. I hated leaving you. I'm sorry. I should have just woken you and brought you. But you were sleeping so well.'

She smiled, jogging about in her saddle. 'The women told me it was the sun. Can you believe it? I've never been so cold in my life. I feel like I've risen from the dead.' She blew him a kiss.

The rest of the morning he felt like someone who had received news of a deserved but unexpected prize. Relief at her recovery, the good fortune of having a photographer along after all, and this extraordinary troop that was surely a hundred years out of date – everything was falling into place. Not only that, but here he was with a woman he loved for whom the whole expedition was every bit as good as it was for him: he didn't feel in the least held back. It was as if he no longer needed to strive to avoid anything, there was nothing to avoid.

15

The operation was a simple one. It occurred in the early afternoon. Up ahead, riders had begun to dismount.

Everyone pulled up, and there was more talking now as people walked about between the camels. The scene reminded Mortimer of a livestock market he had once seen while on assignment with the BBC in the Yemen: the men conversing rapidly, smoking, chewing qat, and the animals standing about chewing the cud, emitting a bellow now and then. Some of the camels decided to sit, others stood waiting to see what would happen. One group of men got a fire going, and blue enamel teapots appeared on the sand, along with dusty plastic bags of tea. Jean Baptiste seized Mortimer's camel by its neck rope. As it bent down Mortimer slipped and found himself hanging by one leg. Baptiste hurried round and disengaged him. He landed heavily on his side, with a strong set of bony fingers digging into his armpit. Savage pins and needles sparked up his legs, and his feet were completely dead, but he was unharmed.

Celeste flipped herself off her mount.

After a glass of tea, Jean Baptiste led them up a dune. Mortimer walked easily for the first time in days: his feet had begun to heal. From the crest of the dune the sand dropped away in furrows, down to a plain that stretched to the horizon. The one visible feature of the plain was a faint white line drawn right across it. Baptiste gestured to the left, and Mortimer picked out a wisp of dust many miles off. He stared and saw that the little dust cloud was moving: a blue funnel of smoke, as if something were burrowing just under the surface along that white line, throwing up a blue exhaust cloud.

'They will have to be quick,' Jean Baptiste muttered.

Mortimer assumed he was referring to whatever vehicle was barrelling down that distant track.

Elsewhere something small fluttered on the plain: a piece of plastic catching the sun, perhaps.

Jean Baptiste fumbled in his robe and pulled out a large pair of binoculars. He made a brief attempt to disentangle the strap from his shesh, but it was too much trouble. Mortimer leaned close, catching a sweet, thick animal whiff of the man, as he brought the lenses against his eyes and tried to find the image, then to steady it. In the midst of a grey circle was the little thing that fluttered. Then it vanished. Then he saw it again.

'*La police*,' Jean Baptiste said.

Mortimer saw that it was a flag at the end of a pole.

'*La frontière*,' Jean Baptiste told him.

'The border?' He made out a low building with a steel roof, and a second building, all but indistinguishable from the land.

'It's the last post. Then in six hours, Mauritania.'

Mortimer swept the binoculars to the left, till he found the travelling object: there was the trail of blue dust, and at the head of it, gleaming like a beetle, a small black thing trembling as it moved.

'They go for supplies once a week,' Jean Baptiste said. 'We should have moved out earlier.'

Mortimer was about to hand back the binoculars when he saw something else: two tiny black figures just below the edifices, then three more, then a little cluster of them: a platoon of diminutive black stick figures, ants on the plain. He tried to hold the heavy binoculars steady for long enough to get a proper look, then handed them back, and used his naked eye. He could just make them out, a little group of black riders, a vanguard. At this distance, on such a vast plain, it was impossible to tell how far they might be from the police buildings: half a mile or less, or perhaps as much as two miles. The land was so flat, so broad and empty, you just couldn't tell.

But it wasn't long before a crackle reached Mortimer's ears. It sounded like someone stepping on dry twigs. Then it came again: another footfall.

A few other Tuareg had joined Baptiste at the brow to survey the proceedings. The black figures below disappeared. The little burrowing animal on the plain had ceased to burrow. Mortimer could see no sign of it at all, as if it had never been there, or had taken itself underground. The ghost of dust had vanished.

In a while the black figures emerged again from wherever they had been. They stood motionless a long time. Then Mortimer perceived that they had spread along the white line on the plain. In another moment they had detached themselves from the line, dropped below it. Then they vanished again.

'*C'est bien,*' Jean Baptiste said.

'What is the police post called?' Mortimer asked. 'How many people man it?'

These were the details he ought to be getting. What had he been thinking lately? Where had he been? He knew nothing: how many were in their own column; was there in fact a leader, and who was he; who was the mullah who had visited in the night; where did he come from; who were the riders with them that weren't Tuareg – among all the black-robed men rode quite a few who wore blue and white robes. He reflected how much information one could ordinarily count on being given as a journalist. Often you did little more than relay information you had yourself received in a succinct summary.

This story was as raw as it got. He had been given virtually nothing except a bit of background.

They shuffled back down to the resting camels. Jean Baptiste arranged more tea for them.

'*Voilà*,' he said. 'It has begun.'

Mortimer kept glancing up at the brow of the dunes but missed the return of the warriors.

Later, Jean Baptiste adjusted his robes and conducted Mortimer to a group among which sat three men in green Algerian police uniforms. Two of them sat chatting with the rebels, drinking glasses of tea, smoking cigarettes, and seemed agitated but not unfriendly, nor uneasy. The third lay on the sand nearby with his arm over his face.

When they all set off Mortimer saw that each of these policemen rode on his own camel. The troop must have brought spares. Yet he hadn't noticed any earlier. Nor, apart from the fact that their three camels were roped together, was there any visible means to detain the captives. He guessed it was unnecessary in the desert.

One of them had a dark stain down one whole side of his khaki shirt. Mortimer noticed his head bowing as he rode, and he slumped forwards as if barely awake. Then he fell off. His fall made two clear thuds over the sibilance of the walking hoofs. He grunted, then lay there silently. After that, a fighter rode pillion behind him, holding him.

The sun hung low: a bronze coin just above the skyline of smooth orange hills, burnished. Time of day meant nothing to these men. Celeste rode beside Mortimer, the late sun shining on her face, turning her skin the colour of the enflamed sand. She smiled at him. In her white robes and headscarf she looked like some heroine from the pages of a Victorian romance. He could sense the bones in her arms, their strength and dryness. Out here, all creatures seemed dry, set free of the need for moisture, released into an existence where no water weighed them down. It was as if here the human body was drained of all excess, and found its true home among the minerals.

There was more talking now than there had been on the way out, as they rode back through a moonlit night. The sand kicked up around the camels' hoofs, pale in the dark like spray round the ankles of a barefoot walker in a beach's shallows. The day's work was done. Mortimer realised he had not eaten since dawn, and hunger had not troubled him at all. Peace tingled in his limbs. He could not remember ever feeling so good. The desert spread out in all directions. They rode its waves like a fleet of war canoes at leisure beneath the cool tent of night.

16

For three days they had the house to themselves. Twice a day a woman brought a bowl of couscous with vegetable stew. The first time she came Mortimer gave her a bundle of dinars; she accepted them without comment and put them inside her robe. The next time she came, she set the same notes down on the sand beside the new bowl of food. There was to be no payment, evidently. But whether that was by force of hospitality or because Mortimer and Celeste were thought to be offering them a service, he never knew.

Other than that woman, they saw few people. Each dawn and dusk Celeste would go out with her camera and Mortimer would either doze, if it was morning and she had left a warm strip for him to roll into in their narrow bed, or else catch up on his notes. He wrote out rough drafts of three stories: an account of what he had seen happen, with a little background; a piece on the history of the Tuareg such as he had gleaned it, and how their way of life was the only one truly suited to the desert; and some fragmentary speculation on the potential involvement of other parties interested either in discomfiting Algeria, or exploiting the Sahara. If he could nail any of that down, it could amplify the story enormously.

Mortimer found a house at the end of the row opposite theirs where a woman would give him a trowelful of hot coals and a pot of tea first thing. He hated to start the day without tea. He copied the locals, alternately letting the pot heat on the embers, and working up a froth by pouring back and forth into a glass, with a hunk of sugar dissolving in it. He'd sit on the edge of their bed sipping from the hot glass, and get to work on his notes. In the ideal world he'd be able to file three stories in one go, as soon as they reached a phone, though in reality he'd most likely have to make a lot of changes. The hardest part was not being able to interview anyone. He only saw Jean Baptiste once in those three days, and he assured Mortimer that he would let him know of any developments. He also said he'd think about who Mortimer might interview, though he never came up with anyone but himself.

Mortimer and Celeste spontaneously occupied the little house as if it were their own. To be contained within their own four walls of mud, to be left alone there, to have this temporary home that was nominally theirs, and see their things scattered about it – Mortimer loved the way they so readily made a home, occupied the house together. To be alone in it, working, knowing Celeste would be back soon but meanwhile was busy at her own work, bolstering his endeavours with hers, felt like a blessing. When she returned he'd pass her a glass of tea, fill the pot and heat up more. There wouldn't be any food till mid-morning. Sometimes they grappled with one another before it arrived. They'd cover themselves with a sheet of beige cotton and make quiet, intoxicating love. He'd smother her cries with his mouth. The heat of her body first thing, the sun outside, the sandy floor, the earth walls, the taste of her lips – all these things seemed to belong together.

For hours at a stretch he'd forget altogether about the newspaper. Once he said to her: 'All day I have hardly thought about work. About the news, television, radio, what we think we are doing here.' He could have asked

Hamed to bring back his battery so they could switch on the radio again, but strangely he had no desire to.

She smiled. 'This is real life. The journalist is always looking for meanings, reading between the lines, interpreting, mistrusting. What happens if for a moment you take things at face value? Look at this place. Yes, things are going on back in Algiers or wherever that could affect it, but these people are just living. Not the fighters but the villagers. They're not thinking about what goes on behind the scenes, they're thinking about the scene in front of their eyes. Will there be enough flour for the children's birthday treat. Can I get home from the gardens an hour early. Will the lettuces come up. Will the rice arrive in time. All the normal day to day bullshit. Except it's not bullshit. We're so busy trying to figure out the story behind things. What if there is no story? Do you ever think about that?'

He had to admit he didn't. 'But everyone's like us,' he said. 'Everyone is busy thinking about the next move.'

'I met a Tibetan lama once. He wasn't. You should have seen just the way he drank a cup of tea. There was nothing else in the whole world but that cup of tea. It's marvellous to watch. It makes you feel – that life is simple. That whatever makes you happy is right. That there's nothing else worth striving for. And then you go outside, and for a little while it stays with you, that feeling. I remember looking around at the trees, the cars with the sun glinting on them, the mountains above Pau shining with snow, and thinking: wow, this beauty – I really felt it for once. And I thought, this beauty is here all the time. Not just now because I happen to have had tea with a Tibetan wise man who is visiting Europe, but all the time. One could always feel this good. And I think those lamas do. They make it their life's work to feel good. Can you beat that?'

He stirred his fingertips through the sand of the floor. 'We want to interpret, understand.'

'But what if there is nothing to understand? I mean –' She leaned forwards and picked up her glass of tea, cooling in the sand, blew steam off the surface. 'Not the way we think. One day, I want to stop all this, do something real. Stop moving all the time.'

He couldn't help frowning. 'This isn't real?' Then he managed a smile. 'Family portraits in a small town in south-west France?'

'There's nothing wrong with that. We all belong among our own people.'

He was going to say something but hesitated.

She smiled and touched his hand. 'Your own people are who you make them. Whoever you love, you should be with them. But in a community, that's what I mean. Working with others, I don't know, to make life good. Better. Trying to do something. Not just watching, observing, seeing others make all the mistakes. One should make mistakes of one's own.'

'We don't do that?'

She thought a moment. 'Not really. Travellers never really get their hands dirty.'

'But we're not just travellers.'

'Observers then. We watch, and comment, and judge. It's easy to when you're not part of anything.'

'I try not to judge,' he said.

Her face creased in a smile. 'I know you do.' She leaned towards him and kissed his forehead. 'But still, what does it all actually consist of, day by day, hour by hour? Travelling. Being in foreign places. Getting on planes, walking around cities we don't know, crossing country we don't know. We think it's all about covering important events, but that's just our pretext.'

Mortimer was silent a moment. 'Maybe you're right. But I don't care, this is the life I want. Especially with you.'

He glanced at her, and for the first time saw a remoteness in her face, as if she were looking at him from a distance. She let out a little laugh, and moved closer to hug him.

He frowned. 'Anyway, how can all this violence keep our hands so clean?'

'We don't compromise. Sure, sometimes in work an editor wants this or that changed a way we don't like. But not really, not in our hearts.'

He knew that right now it was true: there was no compromise in his heart. He was functioning like a well-oiled machine, doing exactly what he had been designed to: roam the lands reporting on the upheavals seizing them, and to be in love. A rush of elation, but tinged with anxiety, or with anticipation, ran through him. Love without hesitation or reservation, love without doubt – he knew that it must be a privilege to feel it, but right now it felt like a birthright.

One night, very late, just before dawn, he went out into the dark village, needing to pee. A late moon hung above the dunes at the end of the little row of houses. It had a few days to go before it would be full.

Far away a man started to sing the early prayers, making his voice resonate so it sounded as though it was coming from a megaphone. He reached the peak of a scale and held his note, then dropped it; and again began low down, working his way upwards. He was singing the name of God. Seeing the band of shadow at the side of the moon, you could almost feel the globe hanging out there in space, not too far from this globe; and also sense the ball of fire that hung in space a long way away, whose light illuminated most of that bright ball. To hear God's name then, uttered by the throat of one of His creatures, seemed entirely appropriate. Whatever balancing act this machine of His was, with its many self-suspended spheres, what could be more natural than to sing one's praise? In that one word the human chest seemed to find a way to encompass the scale of creation.

Mortimer asked himself why it was special with Celeste, and how he knew. He had no good answers. It was almost a physical pain, still, a cramp in the belly. He could never get enough of her physical proximity. He wanted to be next to her, or else talking to her, all the time. This feeling that was both a yearning and a satisfaction, a hunger and a happiness, filled his limbs. He had not known a person could get this way. It was as if his cranium filled with sunlight, as if he could already feel the scope of his future with her. It might well get worse, there would no doubt be troubles, but he wanted to go through them, ride whatever ups and downs being with her brought. He was ready to pledge himself, something that he had never wanted to do with Saskia, even though he had once.

But everything had been different with Saskia. Not just her version of femininity, which seemed to hold attractiveness almost something of which to be ashamed; not just her rushed, heated, but ultimately separate lovemaking, always conducted with the eyes closed. Even her version of morality was nothing like Celeste's. Celeste seemed to act if anything out of a desire to help people; whereas with Saskia it had seemed more a desire to bring down the bad people, and the doing of good was a duty. Her moral valour didn't fill him with aspiration but weighed on him, made him feel not up to the mark. It had got him down more and more.

Hamed had not come on the expedition and ever since, his behaviour towards Mortimer had changed. Instead of humouring him with overuse of the word *monsieur*, he spoke less now, and looked at Mortimer as if hoping to find some answer in his face.

One evening Hamed invited them to his garden. It lay a quarter of a mile away through palm groves, a square of raked earth the size of a suburban swimming pool. There wasn't a weed in sight among rows of young plants. Up above stood the palms, with clusters of dates like bunches of grapes forming under their crowns. The water that enabled the palms to grow, and the shade the trees offered, were the two conditions of the garden. A diminutive canal six inches wide and bone dry ran alongside, with neat little parapets of clay, as straight as if marked out with a ruler. From it an even smaller channel no wider than a cigarette pack ran to the pool in the centre of Hamed's plot. At either end of the pool was a hole with a piece of board set in it: the sluice gates. Tiny clay walls divided the garden into sections. The whole thing was a miniature flood plain, with dykes a couple of inches high, like a model. The miracle of it, other than the fact of its existence here in the middle of the sand dunes, was the perfect horizontal it must have required. Any dip, any slope, would cause the channels to back up and overflow. Mortimer had never seen thrift like it. It was immaculate.

He was about to ask where the water came from when Hamed bunched his robes, tucked them in his belt, and with his mouth open in a grin presented himself to a palm tree. He placed one foot then the other at knee height on the trunk, and commenced to climb in a frog-like action, jumping from one rib of the trunk to the next, rapidly, until he reached the crown, where he pulled the fronds out of his way and with a thrashing of greenery climbed through them. Once on top, he perched there motionless for a moment. Then he opened his mouth and began to sing, sending his voice high into the falsetto range, singing with an urgency, a desperation.

Mortimer clapped and called, 'Encore.'

Another voice could be heard singing far away. Then a third voice answered, not so far away, and after it the distant man sang back. Then Hamed sang again. It went on for fifteen or twenty minutes, the three men singing to one another, perched like birds in the trees above their gardens.

All around lay the dusty land with nothing on it, just the crust of planet stretching away to the horizon. The men's voices seemed to rise out of the very sand and clay of the empty land. It was as if they were singing about the desert, desperate to spread the news not that God was in the desert, but that the desert itself was God.

For a moment it seemed to Mortimer that mankind's existence was the loneliest thing imaginable, a solitary perpendicularity stalking the flat earth with no possible notion as to why it was there. Yet in his sadness there was also a sense of being on the brink of an inner home-coming, one which he recognised probably would not take place, even as he sensed its possibility.

'Come down,' he called softly into the treetop. Celeste's light fingers found his. Her face was deep bronze in the last light. A scarf of weak yellow lay across the west, and beneath it a band of mauve was already spreading up the sky.

17

An aeroplane came the next morning. The tactics were like a giant game of chess. The guerrillas made a move. They went in and collected a pawn off one square. The scale was enormous: squares hundreds of miles broad, and each move might take thirty-six hours or even weeks to effect. Next, the other side sent down a little speck that buzzed in the sky. This winged knight circled over the castle, rolled its wings in friendly fashion, as if giving a wave, then settled on the plain. The home side understood. They sent forth a posse to meet the challenge: a rook perhaps, or a bishop. The two faced each other down. It was a close thing. They brought the knight to the castle for negotiations. Perhaps they could effect a trade of some kind: two pawns for the knight, say.

But it was hard to get to grips when no one would tell him anything, when he had to bob and crane over the shoulders of the two teams crowded round the board to catch a glimpse of the state of play.

Apparently there was not much to see. The party of delegates returned to their aeroplane amid the same escort of camels that had ridden out to meet them. They had landed on the plain of Timimoun. Later, the plane could be heard roaring away through the afternoon. This time it did not buzz the village but pursued a straight course a thousand feet up, droning as it climbed. But something had evidently been achieved. In the middle of the night Mortimer woke to the gurgle of an engine. His first thought was that it must be a generator, though he had seen none in the village. He pulled on his boots.

Lights blazed under the palm trees. He could see the hulk of a vehicle, a Unimog with a canvas top, and beside it a man holding a machine gun. Mortimer was amazed that it could have driven here.

Then Hamed was at Mortimer's side. Before he had a chance to say anything Mortimer put a finger to his lips. Just then a man in an army cap, short sleeves and fatigues, with a military bearing, came walking through the trees, chuckling, followed by two aides. The Unimog had a double-size cab, and they all climbed into it. The great vehicle performed a turn in reverse, then chugged away through the trees, its rear lights picking out the dust in its wake.

Hamed brought food, and they ate in the light of the kerosene lamp. Then he left, and they lay on Celeste's bunk.

'It's actually happening,' Mortimer said. 'A war is starting and we're here to witness it.'

He heard an engine again at dawn, and shook her awake. She drank a quick bowl of water and they went out into the chalky air. At first he thought thin cloud had settled over the oasis, but it was just the pale dawn sky.

The Unimog was back, standing in the same place. This time it was flanked by several camel riders holding up guns. Celeste circled out through the trees with her camera, squinting through it as she went. He heard the rapid, soft clicks, the whining of the automatic wind-on. She was quick about her business.

The camel riders didn't move. Three men climbed down from the vehicle and walked towards the ksar. It wasn't long before they strode back with their heads down, clambered up into the cab and drove away. One or two of the riders turned their mounts to watch them go.

A tussle was evidently going on, without an outcome as yet.

Jean Baptiste came by later with Hamed, who prepared the tea. The situation was that the hostages from the police post, all three of them, were staying.

'It is all we can do for now,' Jean Baptiste said. 'We must make them understand that we are serious. We do not keep our heads in the sand, we know how the world is out there. Why should we not control our piece of it? Why should we not benefit from it? We have told them we might play ball, as you say, but they don't understand. Now we are telling them something else: unless we play ball, there will be no game. But things will become harder now.'

Jean Baptiste blew on his little glass of tea, making the steaming froth lap over the side and on to his fingertips.

The rebels' plan was to perform similar operations in a number of places. It was better to capture than to kill, Jean Baptiste said, not only because desert men preferred not to kill if they didn't have to. Even now in the deep south other bands were executing comparable raids. There had been some fighting, few casualties.

How did he know?

'Radio, of course,' he said, with slight consternation.

So was this headquarters?

He wouldn't answer. He sipped the froth off his tea glass and mimed smoking. Mortimer offered him a cigarette. He smoked it in silence. Halfway through he said, 'Much has yet to be decided. You ask the same questions we are asking ourselves.'

A certain feeling had been dogging Mortimer. Now he recognised it as impatience. It was time, past time, to get to a telephone. He had to get on to Kepple, organise things properly. There was the possibility of using the guerrillas' radio, he supposed, but it was hard to imagine how to contact London with it, if they'd even let him try. Perhaps they could contact a telephone operator somewhere, through whom he could make a call. It seemed highly doubtful. On the other hand, if he found a way of leaving in order to get to a telephone, what might he miss while he was gone? Like the light of stars, news of this war would have to arrive late. News was always late anyway, even at the best of times.

Where did they plan to go next?

Again Jean Baptiste was uncertain, evasive.

'I need a proper contact, that's the problem,' he told Celeste.

'We've stumbled on to this by accident,' she said. 'That's the problem. And the luck.'

'There's Rio Camello next door, Mauritania have already given up their claim on the Western Sahara, and now this. The whole desert could be repartitioned,' Mortimer mused.

In a sense all the borders in the region were notional anyway. The Tuareg came and went as they wished between Mali, Niger and Algeria. If there was a natural country in the heart of the Sahara, it was a Tuareg state. The idea wasn't so implausible. They could probably muster a population of a quarter million, more than in some African countries. And if there really was oil, even if there was only the natural gas that had already been found, they'd have enough of an economic base to boost the domestic product well past Africa's poorest. They'd need friends, obviously, but Jean Baptiste said they had friends. There was one obvious candidate for support: Algeria's long-time rival, Morocco. There would be a kind of justice in the two countries each financing a proxy war against the other: Algeria had the Rio Camello, Morocco would have the Tuareg.

Different men stopped by the house. Some merely wanted to drink a glass of tea with the foreign journalists, smoke their cigarettes; others wanted to preach, imagining perhaps that their words would be broadcast to the world. But none of them would tell Mortimer what the immediate strategy was. Had there been demands, had they been refused? No one would tell him anything. It was maddening. Mortimer scribbled everything down he could think of, but how was he to convey any of it to where it mattered? He would have to make a break for it, get Celeste's pictures and some copy filed soon. But he still needed more interviews.

And that was still a problem, evidently. One morning Hamed took an interminable time finding Jean Baptiste, and when he eventually did bring him, and Mortimer once again requested an interview with a leader, Baptiste tutted and shook his head. He kept on tutting, lightly, then sucked from a glass.

Mortimer changed tack. 'I've got to get to Timimoun anyway,' he said.

Jean Baptiste glanced at him in surprise. Then he shrugged. 'All things are possible.'

He said something in Arabic to Hamed, who at once shook his head.

'This is boring,' Mortimer said aloud to Celeste.

'No, this is as exciting as it gets.'

She was right. He knew she was right. And in fact it all began again soon.

18

They talked until late. She had been at the front line a few times before. 'You keep out of the way,' she said. 'There is no line. It's a mess. No one knows what's going on. Gradually, or suddenly, it becomes clear it's over, and you get to see what happened.'

She lay on her back staring at the ceiling. '*La plus belle des choses*,' she began, then rolled towards him. 'You know that? Sappho. For some the most beautiful sight is a regiment of infantry, or a fleet at sea; but for her it's to see two people in love.'

The battle would have taken place the next day. More riders kept arriving that night, and it was with a battle-yell of ululation that the camel troop set sail at dawn. But a khamsin blew up in the morning. No one could stand up, not even the camels. The Tuareg closed the eye-slits in their veils and settled down to hibernate beside their dethroned mounts. Everyone hid their face as best they could. Mortimer's trousers rode up his ankles as he hunkered down, and afterwards a band of skin was worn raw, as if he had been manacled. The khamsin blew hard for two hours, then became weaker and intermittent, but it was enough to delay things for that day.

They slept out in the dunes. It was bitterly cold. Celeste huddled against Mortimer, until the two of them followed the Tuareg's example and pressed themselves against one of the camels. It turned its head, curious, and its belly groaned noisily.

Mortimer fell in and out of sleep all night. Each time he found himself awake, he heard deep, low voices.

At one point he woke to find the weather had passed entirely, leaving a night of perfect stillness. The shapes of the dunes all around were colourless, dark grey in the night, and the sky was bursting with swollen stars. The stars were so close you'd think they were not more than a hundred feet up; or less, much less, that you could reach up and strum your fingers through them, and they'd swirl about like blossoms on a pond.

Celeste was quite still at his side. Without moving at all, without looking at her, he realised that he knew she was wide awake; and at that moment he too became wide awake.

She was staring at him, her eyes gleaming in whatever little sheen they picked up from the stars.

'After this,' she said softly, not whispering but talking in a low murmur. 'I'm thinking what will happen after this.'

'Taillot said the government will be good to the Tuareg. Too many people like them.'

She hadn't shifted her gaze from him, her eyes both restful and alert. 'I mean when we leave here. I mean us.'

A faint alarm ran through him, though he couldn't have said what exactly he feared, except to be drawn out of the present circumstances, for all their danger. He didn't like to be reminded that the two of them would not always be here in the desert as they were now.

He said, 'It's up to us.'

She pressed her face into his shoulder. He shifted his arm so it was partly round her. He could feel her slender shoulder blade, her ribs, which seemed fine and delicate as a wishbone just then, and precious.

There was no wake-up call. Mortimer lifted his head and saw that nearby a number of camels had got to their feet, and that people were walking about on the sand. Jean Baptiste appeared with a trowel of glowing embers, bedded them in the sand and made tea. It was still dark when the column mounted.

At this hour Mortimer noticed the bittersweet reek of the camels. The riders fell into single file. Mortimer watched the swaying of Celeste's camel in front of his, its haunches sinking from side to side as it climbed the dunes.

Someone had known precisely where they were when they stopped the previous evening. At the top of the first rise the plain of Timimoun opened out pale before them. They filed down the last flank of sand and broke into a trot on the flat land, breaking out of single file and spreading wide. They were clearly heading for the town. Mortimer thought it would surely take them an hour to reach, but it all happened much faster. Instead of the pace slackening it intensified. Soon it became a canter, and Mortimer had to cling to his pommel with both hands. The great neck in front of him sawed back and forth, and there seemed a gulf before him. He dreaded falling and being left behind, and didn't dare look to see where Celeste had got to, though he wanted to.

Someone let off a gun. Mortimer saw palms ahead, and through them the dark wall of the town. The ground had become chalky white, the sky a dull grey. More guns sounded, there was no letting up, in a moment the whole troop was flowing under the trees and along the foot of the town wall. They galloped to the end of it, then circled out onto the plain, doubling back in a broad curve, and came to a halt a hundred yards off.

Mortimer discovered Jean Baptiste and Celeste either side of him, as if he alone had been unable to keep track of the others' movements. The great gates of the town slowly opened. The troop began to ululate, some stepped forward. A group of locals came running out on foot, and a number of riders called out, *hut-hut-hut*, tapping their mounts on the shoulder, and trotted into the town. Not long after, a gang of riders emerged with eight policemen walking between them with their hands on their heads.

Timimoun was then effectively theirs. It was so simply and harmlessly done that the whole procedure might have been nothing more than some annual ceremony. There was gunfire behind the walls, but it was just celebratory, Mortimer guessed. Some of the riders who had remained outside cocked and raised their guns, then shot them into the sky.

It was an easy victory, and a small one. The town only had a handful of representatives of the state, and a couple of thousand inhabitants. The only casualty was a rebel who lost his fingers when his gun misfired during the celebrations.

It was also a short-lived victory. The police had evidently got a message off before they were seized. Not an hour later a Chinook crawled by overhead, its twin fans turning so slowly Mortimer would have sworn he could see them revolving. The rotors thudded like mortar-fire. Once, a beat of the engine cracked like a shell exploding nearby, as the sound ricocheted off the town wall. The helicopter circled the town then droned heavily away.

Its appearance provoked much shouting and letting off of guns, but nothing that couldn't still have fallen within the remit of some elaborate ritual.

The rebels were pragmatists. They departed before the end of day with their prisoners, riding back across the plateau to the relative safety of the dunes.

At dawn three Sikorskys flew in. Mortimer watched them through Jean Baptiste's binoculars from the brow of a dune. They either landed or went away. Without a second thought, it seemed, the rebels mounted and made their way swiftly across the pan of clay, back towards the town. Jean Baptiste held back Mortimer and Celeste for a while, then agreed to allow them within half a mile of the town, and they all galloped off after the troop. They watched from a dry wadi while sporadic gunfire crackled and wisps of smoke drifted in the sky. The helicopters evidently hadn't left. One of them appeared, flying right over the town. It made a hurried descent, and as soon as it touched the ground just outside the walls, jumped back into the air, whereupon it was engulfed in flame, and black smoke poured from beneath the rotor. A moment later it sank down slowly, heeled on to one side, and Mortimer then heard the boom of its landing.

Celeste had been snapping with her long lens, and now scurried out on foot for a better angle. Jean Baptiste shouted after her. She called back that she was all right, but didn't look round or stop.

Not long after, the two unscathed helicopters droned away to the east, and Celeste returned. The three of them remounted and rode slowly towards the town.

Celeste had ushered three of the riders towards the stricken helicopter, and had them pose on their camels before it, guns held over their heads.

'They'll like that shot,' she muttered to Mortimer afterwards, as she was labelling the film.

19

The grenade looked like something from the pages of the *Commando* comics Mortimer had read as a boy, an old Jerry stick grenade with a cap on the end. It came rolling out of the town gate and tapped against one of the giant wooden doors. No one ever established who had thrown it, or why. It wasn't unknown for grenades to be part of celebrations among the tribesmen. Or boys might have got hold of it, Jean Baptiste thought.

It happened just after Mansour, the big Egyptian doctor, came strolling up the road, a stately figure under the palms, gliding between them and the wall in his long white kaftan, his face with its thick moustache looking serious in the sunlight.

He shook Mortimer's hand. 'You are back in time to see our *news*,' he said, and nodded at Celeste, who was busy photographing a group of boys playing with a gun. 'You can tell them about this back in London.'

Mortimer at once felt calmer and clearer in the man's company.

'I hope the desert was good to you,' he said. When he looked at Mortimer with his slightly sad-looking bright eyes, and stood close to him, something went quiet in Mortimer's breast.

'My colleagues are frantic. Now they want to go home more than ever. I tell them that now more than ever we will be needed.'

He walked on towards the town gates with the calm interest of a landowner making the daily round of his property, hands behind his back. Mortimer saw him pause at the gate thirty yards away, and engage a boy in conversation. Then the boy ran off, and the grenade appeared, rattling across the dust.

Mansour stood there alone beneath the high arch as it rolled towards him.

There was a split second when Mortimer knew what was going to happen, long enough for him to feel the ground tilt. When it detonated a group of men standing fifty yards off jumped. The crash seemed inordinately loud, and the sound ricocheted off the town wall as if being answered by further explosions timed to go off one after another. The men quickly realised they were safe and it was just some piece of celebration going on, and turned to look without moving, covering their momentary alarm by standing still.

Mansour had gone. A puff of smoke lingered, as of a car that had had trouble getting started, and one of the town gates had lost a ragged bite from its corner. At least a yard of lumber had been blown off. Then Mortimer saw Mansour lying on his front against the foot of the wall. The side of his kaftan was already dark, and on his back the cloth was dusty and dirty.

It took five of them to carry him into a house just within the walls. Someone whipped up a rug and they laid him on his back on the earth floor. Already there was a bad smell, the sweet, fetid smell of offal.

Mansour's face was smeared with dirt but seemed otherwise unscathed, but his chest was in a terrible state. His kaftan had been cut up, revealing a dark glinting mess within. Mortimer held his breath and did not look closely. He ran off to fetch another of the Egyptian doctors.

The only one he could persuade to come was a tall, balding man who was walking around the yard outside his house, glancing towards the town centre with round eyes, and muttering to himself, shaking his head. In spite of his obvious fear he agreed to come and quickly fetched a bag of supplies.

By the time they got to him Mansour's face had turned yellow and there was a dazzled air in the room that Mortimer recognised at once as the presence of death. The doctor shook his head and said there was no need to examine him, though he did so anyway. They covered him with a headscarf.

'*Ça va?*' A man caught Mortimer's elbow. It was Jean Baptiste. '*Tu vois*, another operation. Small but successful.' He pulled Mortimer away.

Mortimer stood in the doorway, in the shade of the building, just outside the glare of the brilliant day. It was late morning, very hot. The sand of the village was blinding, almost white. Across it fell the stripes of palm shadows. Palms and sand, palms and sand: the material of hot countries. He would often be among them now. Just now he remembered he liked a hot country: when he arrived in one, it was as if he pulled on some old and trusted jacket, a second skin.

He hadn't noticed Celeste in the room. She came out now, shaking her head. He put an arm round her, and she said nothing, but kept on shaking her head. Then she exhaled sharply, as if on the point of tears. 'I'm sick of this. Sick of stupid, stupid killing. For what?' She shrugged him off. 'I get hold of my camera, you get your notebook, and we think it's all so important. We don't see that we are the problem.'

Mortimer's chest was a furnace. He felt he needed to be moving, needed a breeze to cool it down. But what he needed most urgently was a telephone: that was all he could think about.

'They've smashed their radio,' Jean Baptiste told him. 'They don't want word to get out.' He looked seriously at Mortimer. 'You must be careful.'

If he didn't get to a phone today someone might hear

of this and beat him to it, and all their work could end up going to waste. They needed to courier up Celeste's films too, preferably today. 'I have to get back to El Menia,' Mortimer said.

Jean Baptiste tutted. He stood tall, gazing out of the gate across the flat plain, which just now was the colour of chalk. The dunes in the distance at the far side were pink. A little way out a number of men and boys stood in a respectful line, near the fallen helicopter.

'You can't go that way. There will be roadblocks and they could shoot at anything that comes.'

'But I must get to a phone. Or else it's all useless, a waste of time.'

'You will go the other way.'

'But there's nothing the other way.'

'*Si*,' he frowned. 'The frontier. Morocco.'

'Morocco?'

'Four hours, less in a good truck.'

Mortimer's mind clouded. He hadn't contemplated going into another country.

'But how will I find you again?'

And what might happen while he was gone? On the other hand, he had enough already for at least three pieces, he was sure of it, if not four, and time was of the essence. Any day a television crew might drop in out of nowhere, and he'd lose everything, all the surprise and momentum behind the ambush of the front page. Because that was where he was heading, he realised, surprised both to discover that this had been his secret hope all along, and that it felt like a real possibility now.

'They will negotiate now,' Jean Baptiste said. 'We believe so. It may be quiet for a little while.'

It seemed implausible to Mortimer that the Algerian government would permit a handful of rebels to take control of a town, even a small one, and not seize it right back. But then Jean Baptiste said something strange.

'You must talk to Taillot. We have promised him. He has helped us and we have agreed. He has to know what you will print.'

'What do you mean? What's it got to do with Taillot?'

Jean Baptiste sucked through his teeth. 'It's difficult. He might be involved.'

'Involved?'

'Elf Aquitaine, they are our friends.'

Dimly Mortimer recognised that he was being told something unexpected, which would solve a number of riddles that had previously preoccupied him, before he had got caught up in the exotic adventures of the past few days.

'Please,' Jean Baptiste went on. 'Talk to Taillot.'

Mortimer nodded.

'You must not print anything without talking to him. We have to know what the reaction will be once the news gets out. The government might decide to send in everything they have. Taillot is our one sure friend. We have given our word that Elf Aquitaine can have the contracts, if we succeed.'

Again Mortimer nodded, hearing the words as if they were being uttered to someone else, and recognising that they were the key he needed.

'If, or once, the Tuareg state is established,' Jean Baptiste was saying, 'that is the first thing we must do, get the oil flowing, with Elf's help.'

20

A tanker truck had arrived the night before down the track from El Menia, and was travelling on to the border. It was the best they could do, a small dirty tanker which had perhaps once been white.

The driver, a fat man, his belly spilling out from under the hem of his T-shirt, folding over the waist of his trousers, slowly rolled out of town, with much churning of gears and hissing of the compression switch. He hadn't shaved in a good few days and his hands were grimy with oil.

'*La frontière?*' he asked, and cocked his head.

The radio screeched. It was a moment before Mortimer realised over the roar of the engine at their feet that the sound it made was music, some frantic Arabic concoction. The driver bounced on his seat, ignoring the potholes, crashing right through them. Except once when he braked hard and flipped through the gears, then wound off the tarmac, ground along the piste beside it for a hundred yards, bypassing a stretch holed with craters the size of cars.

He reached down and pulled a thermos from under his seat, splashed out a cup of thin grey liquid, which he held out past Mortimer to Celeste.

She took a sip then handed it to him. It was warm,

spicy. He drank a little and handed it back to the driver. The man drained it in one go, then removed his hands from the steering wheel and mimed driving. 'Land-Rover? You don't have Land-Rover?'

Mortimer shook his head.

The driver grinned at him. 'Where are you going?'

'The coast.'

'*Pas bon,*' the man said. 'You should bring your own Land-Rover. You can't cross the desert like this. If you do, the drivers will take you and do bad things to you. Or to your woman.'

The man was silent a while. '*Il faut faire attention.* There are bad people.'

As long as they didn't stop, Mortimer thought, they'd get through this ride all right.

It was afternoon when they reached the border village. It was a small place of low mud homes, one of which, bare inside except for a table and two chairs, was the border post itself. The official, a man in trousers and shirt rather than the local cotton robe, but otherwise no uniform, or anything else to distinguish his office, stamped their passports, copied out their details into a ledger with a blue ballpoint pen, and said wearily, '*Bienvenues en Maroc.*'

There was a grey telephone on the table. Mortimer pleaded and pulled out his wallet, but the man held it up to Mortimer's ear and said, '*Vous voyez?*' The earpiece was stone dead. 'The lines have not worked since September.'

It was around three in the afternoon and fearsomely hot.

You could tell it was another country. For one thing,

there were tin signs tacked to walls advertising Coca-Cola, Goodyear tyres, Marlboros.

The frontier official locked up his office with an aluminium padlock of a kind Mortimer had used on his bicycle as a teenager, and led them down a side street to a yard where a large truck with an enclosed back was parked.

The owner of the truck, a man in red and white robes with a dark purple headscarf, grinned and told them the bus would be leaving in two days for the coast.

'The bus?' Mortimer asked.

The man opened up the back of the truck and gestured at rows of leather straps slung across the interior. This was the bus and these were its seats.

For two thousand francs the man agreed to leave that day. But it was an hour before he had filled up with petrol, then driven around the town blaring his horn, picking up a few passengers who could be heard laughing and chatting as they settled in the interior behind the cab, as if amused by the change in routine. Finally he pointed the bulbous bonnet of the truck out of town, towards the late-afternoon sun.

'Do we have to go to the coast?' Mortimer asked Celeste.

'There's nothing before Tarfaya,' she said. 'I'm sure of it. Nothing at all. Plus we can fly from there, or at least from El Ayoun, which is nearby. We could be in Casablanca tomorrow.'

The sky thickened into a grey pallor. The sun itself appeared as a great red balloon above the level of the plain, and slowly sank into bands of darker and darker red as it approached the very edge of the sheet of land. Soon after it was gone the driver flipped the gear stick into neutral and switched off the engine and let the vehicle coast to a stop.

No need to park, out here on this table top of clay. Where the truck stopped was camp.

Mortimer pleaded and offered him money to keep driving through the night, but the driver wouldn't do it. He tutted and grinned and could not be swayed.

Celeste clutched his hand and told him it would be all right. They would leave at dawn and reach the little city before lunchtime. A few hours could surely not make such a difference.

'And look at this, it's beautiful.'

It was true. A fan of brilliant orange had opened up in the sky. The whole plain had turned mauve. It was incalcuably big. And utterly empty, without blemish.

Celeste's face looked more tanned than ever, a rich nut brown.

The other passengers had come prepared. A man who had brought along charcoal built a fire. A woman kneaded dough in a bowl, dug a pit in the earth and laid three flat loaves in it and sprinkled sand over them. The man then shovelled up his glowing coals and tipped them over the buried bread, and set about making tea.

A star shone so brightly that Mortimer thought for a moment it must be a plane coming in to land. Then more stars appeared, until a snowfield spread across the night.

Mortimer switched on his torch and got to work in his notebook, figuring out how to work in the speculative involvement of an oil company in the insurrection. It was something Kepple would want corroborated, but it was priceless.

They were up early and on the road before dawn. It was good to be driving in the cool, dark air with a hint of dust in the back of the throat. Mortimer's limbs were filled with an early-morning freshness, a feeling of having stolen a march on the world. Soon the sky lightened. They glided along on the rumbling axles over the smooth plain with its mild undulations, and saw it grow from black to mauve. Beneath their feet the engine of the old truck chortled.

After the chilly night it was good too to be in that cab feeling the warmth of the motor. Mortimer was stiff with cold. It was a lovely place to be, high up on the old deep black seats, with the littered iron floor at their feet, and the big windscreen before them with its radial smears of desert dust, and Celeste beside him. There was only water to drink. Mortimer understood in a new way the necessity not so much of coffee or tea but of a hot drink in the morning, especially after such a night of hard, cold ground: it healed the body of night-time.

The driver, who had wrapped his scarf back into place like a turban, offered Mortimer a cigarette. They were a cheap local brand, sweet, sickly blonde tobacco, but he liked it all the same. With Celeste next to him in the cab, with dawn breaking behind them, and a desert breakfast of water and a cigarette, he felt good things in the air.

He thought of the four pieces he had written out and revised again by the light of his torch, and instead of panicking about how to transfer them to where they were needed as soon as possible, for the first time he quietly looked forward to when he and Celeste would roll back into civilisation, and he would be able to settle in a phone kiosk, or by a hotel bed, and spend an hour giving all the pieces to copy. Then there'd be the thrill of the phone ringing and it being Kepple, and all the big machinery of the press would swing into gear in order to take his material and get it out into the world. And this war, all this work he had been at times almost inadvertently, unwittingly doing over the past few weeks, all of it would emerge into the light and become real. It would get on the world's agenda: another problem now known, to be addressed if not solved.

Sure enough, in Tarfaya Mortimer couldn't wait until they'd found a hotel, but went into the first phone boutique he saw, got a pile of change from the old woman who ran it, and ducked into one of the five cabins and pulled the glass door shut after him. Kepple let out a long 'Ah' when he heard his voice, clearly pleased to hear from him, and after a quick exchange of greetings transferred him to the copy-takers, telling him to give them everything he had. He dictated all four pieces, then was transferred back to Kepple, who told him to call back in an hour. Then they took a beaten-up Mercedes taxi to the small, dusty city of El Ayoun, half an hour away, where there was an airline office.

Celeste labelled all her films and sent them to London by Royal Air Maroc's courier service. The next passenger flight out wasn't till Wednesday, three days away, but the films would go on the postal flight that afternoon.

They checked into a new concrete hotel in the centre of town, across the street from a noisy, dusty construction project. The room had a phone by the bed, but when Mortimer picked it up, there was no dial tone, only a faint hiss. Which at least perhaps meant the line wasn't completely dead. He clicked the button a few times, then a man's voice said in slow, lugubrious French: '*Quel numéro vous voulez composer?*'

'Well,' Kepple said when he got through to him, 'you've done it. You're on the front page. Just as soon as the films arrive we'll get them developed and see if we can't get a picture up there too. We'll send a bike out to Heathrow to fetch them. Congratulations. We're going to use everything, all the pieces.'

Mortimer hung up and felt faint. He could hardly believe what he had just heard. Was this really his own life he was leading, and not someone else's?

When he told Celeste she gave him a tight hug and kissed him on the nose.

'And he says he'll try and put one of your pictures on the front page too, once the films arrive.'

She smiled. 'That's nice.'

'Nice? It'll be fantastic.'

She pinched his nose lightly. 'I'm excited for you,' she said, and hugged him again.

They strolled down to the port to find a place for lunch, and sat under an awning at a café-restaurant beside the harbour. They ordered brochettes, couscous, salad, 'Spanch omlet' and two bottles of Fanta, two of Heineken.

The place was deserted except for a middle-aged white couple a few tables away. They got talking. The couple were English, it turned out, from Cornwall. The man, who introduced himself as Colin, had fine, fair hair and blue eyes with tiny pupils, as if they'd seen too much of the sun, and a weathered, wrinkled face. The woman, Vicky, was overweight, with a reddish, puffy complexion and uneasy black eyes.

'What brings you here?' Mortimer asked them.

'See that?' the man said, nodding towards the harbour. 'That's what brought us here.'

'And what's taking us out,' the woman added with a chuckle. 'This afternoon and not a moment too soon, I can tell you.'

'Now now, Vicky,' the man said.

Among the fishing pirogues moored in the muddy water of the harbour stood a white yacht, the bare pole of its mast looking impossibly tall among the local boats.

'They don't call this the dark continent for nothing,' she went on. 'I tell you, I can't wait to see Mount Teide on the horizon. Las Palmas, that's the place for me.

Whatever possessed us to come here I can't think. You'd never believe it's only a hundred miles away.'

'How long will it take?' Celeste asked.

'Twenty-four hours at the outside. We'll be having drinks in the marina tomorrow night,' she said, and giggled nervously.

'What are your plans?' Colin asked. 'Don't suppose you fancy a trip to the Canaries? We've lost our deck hand.'

It was Mortimer's idea. There was no time to think about it – just the momentum of their journey pushing them on.

'We'll get home quicker,' he said. 'From Las Palmas there'll be several flights a day to London and Paris. Come on. And you love sailing.'

As he spoke he was conscious that they needed to talk again about what they were going to do next, where they would go. For the moment, when his stock was high at the paper, he felt he should get back there soon and see if he could consolidate his position.

She shrugged. 'I've never done an ocean trip like that. I hope you don't get seasick.'

They were sitting side by side on the hotel bed. From their fourth-floor window they had a view past a water tank of the blue sea, looking impossibly inviting. It was irresistible. 'I've never been on a sailing boat,' he said. 'Look at that. The ocean. We'll wash the desert right out of our hair.'

'But now?'

'Why not? We are here, the boat is here, they need us. And we can figure out what we're going to do next.'

It was fine enough when they first left port. Mortimer had decided not to take any Dramamine: he'd adjust quicker.

Vicky came bustling out of the companionway past Colin, who was sitting at the wheel in the cockpit. She ripped down a pair of trousers and a T-shirt that were drying on a line, shook her head and hissed at him, 'What are you doing? It was *you* that told *me*.'

She disappeared back down below.

Celeste and Mortimer, seated up on the white fibre-glass deck just in front of the cockpit, on top of the cabin, glanced at one another.

A moment later Colin said: 'It's supposed to be bad luck to leave port with your washing out. I wasn't thinking.'

The couple had been living in their boat for three years, yet it didn't seem to Mortimer that either of them was quite happy about it, as if they were still waiting to discover the point of their life on a yacht, travelling the Caribbean and Mediterranean. In some ways it was as if they had never left home: the main cabin, a sloping-walled chamber with benches all down one side, and on the other a galley, then a built-in desk where the charts and pilot books and single sideband radio were all housed, was covered, walls and floor, in brown carpet. With its few china ornaments, it felt like a particularly cramped English living room. There was a sleeping cabin up at the front where Colin and Vicky had their berth; Mortimer and Celeste would bunk down on the benches.

They left their bags in a cavity underneath the seats, against the sloping fibreglass of the hull.

It was a single-masted boat, a sloop, and not sleek, if anything broad in the beam. All round the big white deck ran railings of plastic-coated cable. There were various winches, handles and cleats all over the deck, and numerous pale, soft ropes: all the age-old technology of sail. At the back was the cockpit with the big chrome wheel in the middle.

Once they were on the boat and getting ready to go, it seemed less of a pleasure cruiser and more like a serious piece of equipment with a job to do. It was workman-like, designed with the purpose of accomplishing a task, not filling leisure hours. Celeste walked around looking at the ropes and winches, touching the mast and gazing up its splendid height admiringly.

The sun was shining and the sea was a rich blue. Sounds of the land dwindled, until all you heard was the running of water along the hull, and now and then a brief rumble of the big red sails. Along the coast the town flattened itself into a single line of white geometry. Here and there a mud-coloured tower rose up, and a palm tree stood with its fronds like a cluster of roots. You could feel the strength in the breeze as the boat heaved to one side. It began to rock. Both to rock and to swivel. It nosed itself downward into each swell, swivelled a little on its keel, and sprang back up, then repeated the move. At first Mortimer was interested by this curious motion, then became aware of a dull fear. Then he belched and felt dizzy. A moment later he was leaning over the side ejecting a hot stream of spicy vegetable soup. He watched it spatter into the blue water and travel quickly out of sight. Another stream poured out of him, and this one hurt his stomach much more than the first. A third smaller eruption came, which hurt still more. Then again his diaphragm clamped itself into a knot, and nothing emerged but a string of black phlegm that swung from his lips over the moving blue water.

When he lifted his face his head was spinning so badly he didn't think he could stand up. He clutched the rail at the side as the deck heaved back and forth under him, pitching this way and that. Every pitch sent a weight rocking back and forth in his skull. He glanced back at the now narrow line of the land, and yearned to get back to it.

Celeste's hand touched his back, and the sensation caused him to retch over the side once more. The boat pitched and again the weight heaved within his head.

When it had eased up enough to speak, he groaned and said he thought he needed the seasickness pills. But he couldn't for a moment imagine going down the ladder into the carpeted box of the cabin to search for them in his bag.

He heard Celeste moving away behind him, and uttered a silent prayer of thanks.

She returned with a mug of water and the little foil-wrapped tray of pills. But every one he took over the next hour jumped back out within a few minutes on a little gush of water, sometimes so soon after he had swallowed them that the water would still be cool.

Celeste shook her head and tutted. 'You don't have to do everything, you know. You don't have to get on a boat just because it's there.'

He groaned.

The rest of the afternoon he lay below with his head wedged against the carpeted wall, and tried to sleep. As long as he didn't move or open his eyes he found he could keep his stomach under control. When Vicky started cooking in the galley a few feet away, he breathed with his mouth open and held his nose. At some point he opened his eyes and saw that night had fallen outside the portholes. Later still he was woken by a bang up above, and felt the boat pitching about more violently. He could hear Colin shouting on deck, and the murmur of Vicky's voice answering him. He wondered if something was wrong and he ought to get up. The banging went on for a while, and one loud boom made the hull shudder. But he couldn't face lifting his head and opening his eyes and rising to his feet. He knew he'd immediately be overcome by nausea and wasn't sure he'd be able to make it to the open air before retching.

When he woke again a low grinding filled the boat, and it was light outside.

Nervously he folded back the blanket someone had thrown over him, feeling chilled and ill, and stiff, and climbed into the cockpit.

Celeste was at the wheel staring contentedly ahead. 'Hey you,' she said. 'Oh la la, you missed all the action.

We're using the engine now. Did you hear that storm in the night? The mainsail ripped to pieces.'

'Ripped?' Mortimer asked, surprised to hear that sails could do that.

'He had it reefed wrong.'

Somehow it was comforting to be travelling under motor. It seemed more familiar.

Mortimer glanced out over the side and immediately felt sick again. A lot of waves seemed to be travelling in all directions rapidly, some of them rushing at the side of the boat, slapping it, then rushing off in some other direction.

'We're going back,' she said. 'So he can get the sail fixed.'

Mortimer groaned and slumped down into the seat beside her and rested his head in her lap. She stroked his scalp. He couldn't remember ever feeling so cared for. Whatever ill assailed him, she would have patience for it, she would understand. She understood him: it was as simple as that. No one ever had before. It was wonderful luck, even while bobbing about on the Atlantic in the grip of nausea.

22

The problems started not with the tearing of the mainsail during the squall in the night, but when Colin pulled out his radio direction finder later in the day, inserted its earpieces in his ears, scanned the horizon with it, then consulted the charts down below, and discovered that they had overshot El Ayoun, and instead were near Dakhla, a port in the very south of the Moroccan Sahara.

Mortimer exulted to hear that they were near any port. It was clear that they would simply make for that one instead, and Colin thankfully agreed. Mortimer was so relieved to be on his way back to land, where he would not only get his feet back on firm ground but also resume his life, now uncomfortably interrupted, that he offered to take the wheel for a spell, and found that while holding the long chrome spokes he could watch the pitching of the prow and feel not the least trace of fear or sickness. Instead, it was exhilarating to have this great body of boat before one. He didn't even notice when land appeared on the horizon. Suddenly there it was: a thin green line and, when they were closer, a thin white line just beneath it.

Nor did he notice time passing. There they were now, not a mile offshore, with a cluster of tiny white shapes visible above the green line, which were houses catching the afternoon sun.

They had to find the mouth of a river that led into the port. According to the pilot book there was a sandbar in the river's estuary, which meant that from sea, even just a few hundred yards out, the line of white surf was uninterrupted. It was hard to spot the precise point where a boat could gain passage into the river mouth.

They could hear the surf now, a faint roar, and Mortimer's exhilaration grew at the sound of it. Then they spotted a water tower mentioned in the pilot book, and Colin decided to head for that. The river mouth should appear as they approached. Finally they saw it, a silvery sheet of smooth water beyond the mist of breakers, and a cluster of smoky-looking palm trees on the end of a spit of land.

To reach the river they had to get through the surf. But Colin wasn't worried. 'She's built for waves,' he said. Plus he'd grown up on the beaches of Cornwall, knew surf inside out.

'Just so long as it's deep enough.'

This made Mortimer feel better still: if the sea here might be so shallow that the boat could even hit the bottom, then they were all but back on land already.

They got busy storing things below, locking up the cupboards, then Colin pointed the prow straight at the stand of palm trees.

Mortimer and Celeste sat on either side of the cockpit, each with a sheet rope Colin gave them, to control the jib-sail at the front. Colin was between them at the wheel. Vicky kept herself below.

The first breaker arrived slowly. It was as if it came to them, and not the other way round. Mortimer realised that a small cliff had opened up under the prow, a drop of ten or twelve feet. This cliff slowly moved down the length of the hull. At a certain point it would reach the midway point, and the boat would fall.

'We should be in bloody harnesses,' Colin said loudly, as if admonishing someone.

The next thing Mortimer knew an avalanche of dazzling white snow was collapsing all around the cockpit.

He looked at Celeste and she was flying high above him with her hair streaming and the blue sky behind her. A moment later she was directly beneath him, inches from dull grey froth. He himself would have dropped right on to her had he not been clutching the rails. Then there was a deep thud that caused the boat to stand still for a moment. Then it was moving again, and all around was a dazzling snowfield of hissing, seething fresh snow.

Celeste had moved. Mortimer looked up the boat but she wasn't there. He shouted to Colin and clambered on to the roof of the cabin, then peered down into the hold. She had vanished.

Colin shouted back and Mortimer jumped across and gripped the shrouds where Celeste had been sitting, and looked out over another sheet of new snow, effervescing in the sunshine. He scanned it frantically, then stared into the green face of a glass wall building itself, pulling itself clear of the brilliant froth, green as an empty wine bottle, tall as a house. He searched the gathering wall, and the emptying trough beneath it, that seemed to get lower and lower, falling away as the battlement of water grew taller. There was no sign of her wherever he looked. Then the boat jarred and shook, and tipped right up so his face was suddenly inches from another collapsing snowfall, and he could feel the spray on his face. Then he was staring at the blue sky, and he had to cling on tight not to drop backwards, and he heard a cry behind from Colin. Then again he was looking across a dazzling waste of snow and there was still no sight of Celeste. Colin was still shouting, repeating something. Then Mortimer saw a shoe travelling through the water at what seemed an unnaturally rapid pace, back towards yet another eminence that was beginning to pull itself from the slanted sheet of white. It was a sneaker, and he recognised its rippled sole under a film of shining water.

He got his legs over the rails and jumped. He judged the leap just right, and at once his hand closed around the shoe. It seemed some kind of start. The water wasn't cold, and he lifted his head to look for her. At once blocks were falling on top of him, and he went under. In a second his ears and nose, his whole head was full of water, and he was in darkness, and a powerful turbulence had got hold of him, and he was being turned round and round. Still he held the shoe in his hand. Already his lungs were burning, his gullet was pumping, and he no longer knew which way the air might be.

Then for no reason he could fathom his head was out of the water. He heard himself gasp and gulp water and gasp again, and saw a tremendous hillside of green moorland streaked with runnels of grey snowmelt coming at him. He turned and lunged flat out away from it, but could get no purchase for the leap, stretched out flat without moving, and felt himself being rapidly sucked right into the very foot of the moving mountain. Once again he was in the roiling darkness. Powerful fish surged past his limbs, knocking them this way and that in their hurry to swarm by. This time he kicked and jerked himself and tried to keep away from them. They turned him over and over and his cheek scraped something like gravel and he heard – strangely, given the boiling thunder all around

– a click deep within his skull, then once again he was mysteriously in the open air. He was out for longer this time, and no wall or mountainside was rushing at him. Instead, behind a far-off ridge he saw a TV aerial, or a white post, or a flagpole tipping first this way then that. Then apparently from nowhere another wall was after him, had stolen right in behind him, and collapsed just before it reached him. He found he was stirring armfuls of dazzling white air as he tried to swim, and again he went down into the darkness and bumped against the gravel, this time with his chest as well as the side of his head, only it was smoother than gravel, and very flat, and he understood that it was sand. When the turbulence had passed he put his feet down and touched it with his foot and at once sprang up, sprang and lunged, and again. The bottom came a little nearer each time. Then he was trying to run, wading and jumping, and he could hear himself gasp and gulp horribly as he jumped and waded, still fighting through the seething and churning white even when it only came to his thighs, rushing to get clear of it before it dragged him back, which with every step it tried to do, to lasso his thighs and hurl him backwards off his feet. Then he stepped suddenly into a deeper pool that came up to his chest, and he sprang up at once choking in fright. Then it was calmer, the noise was further away, the water was still and grey and ruffled with feathery ripples. He pushed through it and again got into shallower water where he could stand easily, and the water was down to his waist once more, then his knees, then it was all but gone. He was wading through ankle-deep mud, watery mud that swirled this way and that carrying froth on its back. He didn't trust it at all, and raced still to get free of it, and got free and at last was standing on a sheen of wet, hard sky.

The noise had moved off now, it had left him alone. He heard a trickle close by, and his right hand grew lighter all by itself. He looked down and saw he was still holding the shoe.

He saw her resting fifty yards away in the shallow waters. She had her face down, she was getting her breath back, so exhausted she didn't even have the strength to lift her face. He started to run towards her and fell over. He got up but his legs were jelly, his trousers heavy, and he stumbled again but kept upright this time, and ran on, stumbling and running, his hands clawing at the wet grey sand each time he nearly fell. He didn't know how he reached her, how he came to be kneeling at her side and struggling to lift her far shoulder and roll her on to her back. It was much harder to do than it ought to have been. Her legs knocked with each line of froth that rushed in towards them, and she groaned where she lay in the grey water with the fan of pale hair like fine hay spread around it. When he got her on her back her arms lay wide apart. Her lips were open and chalky blue. He put his head on her chest, calling out involuntarily. A shudder ran through her and she rolled on to her side under him. Water gushed from her mouth and nose.

It was still too deep here, the ripples splashed over her face. Quickly he got himself behind her head with his hands in her armpits and tugged her up on to the smooth sand gleaming like marble, like varnished wood. There on the smooth polished table of the beach he knelt over her, held her and lifted her on to his thighs. She let out a high-pitched rasp of a choke. He rubbed her sternum, and she began to sob with every breath. He kissed her and undid her shirt, unravelled the long white cotton scarf from the desert that had wound itself round her neck, and kissed her again.

He collapsed next to her with his arms still round her warm, wet body. He closed his eyes and felt nothing but the warm soft weight beside him. She let out a long wail and turned her face into his neck.

Meanwhile, out to sea beyond the rows of white that slowly travelled in, the strange pale boat floated quite still, except for its tall white mast, which tipped back and forth as if waving at him.

He didn't know how long they lay there, on the deserted board of the beach that stretched away empty in either direction. A pile of bushy clouds had congregated over the land to the east, and were brilliant white like steam in the late sun.

The beach shone and turned dark brown like a wet suntan. The clouds grew luminous, streaked with yellow. Still the boat was out there bobbing slightly back and forth.

'I've got your shoe,' he said at last, and his voice felt as though it was being used for the very first time.

She groaned.

Later, a big local fishing canoe sailed past. The men stood up and looked at them and they looked back at the line of six figures in bright yellow oilskins gliding by. Later still, a white Peugeot pickup truck appeared on the brow of the beach and two policemen in brown fatigues climbed out.

The yacht was still there, anchored beyond the surf. The next morning when they came back down it would be gone.

23

They spent two nights in the town of Dakhla on that bleak, deserted coast, waiting for the consular officials to arrive from Casablanca. They had lost everything: her cameras, his notebooks, their wallets, passports, clothes. The British consul tried to arrange a wire of money to a local bank but it never came through. The first night the police gave them cast-off clothing that they were keeping in a box at the back of the station: a pair of crimson jeans for Mortimer, a long green corduroy dress for Celeste. They stood together in a storeroom rubbing themselves down with thin towels, and pulled on the baggy clothes and looked at each other and laughed. It was the first time they had, since they had dragged them-selves out of the sea. Celeste had hardly looked at him all that time. For just a moment Mortimer felt a flicker of relief: they had been through the adventure to beat all adventures, and survived, and were still together. But he saw her face darken again, and his own fear came back. They were lucky to be here. There was nothing good about it. It was fearful. He held her against him in her stiff unfamiliar dress, and she stood quite still.

The police gave them a plate each of couscous with meat stew. Four of them sat around in their sand-coloured uniforms while Mortimer and Celeste ate at a desk seated on steel chairs.

The whole town was bleached by the season of sand-storms. Dust coated everything. Palm trees, hoardings, houses, concrete blocks, the Peugeot trucks parked at the roadside, even the few people on the streets, everything was blighted by dust, faded to the colour of cloud.

There was a hotel with one star, a bleak modern building where the police put them up. The room had a telephone but it didn't work. There was water in the bathroom, and they both showered, and came out with the taste of dust in their mouths. A woman scrubbed out his shirt, and it came back smelling of dust.

Mortimer tried to apologise for having insisted they get on the boat. 'It was a terrible idea. It was no fun being sick, for a start. Then I nearly get us killed.'

'*I* do,' she corrected.

'We should have just relaxed at the hotel for a couple of days, then flown.' Yet even though he said that, he could feel that deep down he was happy to have had that experience: not just to know what it was like to be out on a small boat on the ocean, but to have experienced so intimately the huge force of the waves. It was another of the marvels of the world that you would never encounter unless you packed your bag and headed out.

He didn't so much feel guilty as sad to see Celeste so scared and defeated.

She didn't sleep. In the middle of the night he woke to find her sitting up in bed hugging her knees. He clicked on the lamp, which gave out a dim, yellow glow.

After a while she said, 'I'm going home. I'm sick of being on the road. I've had enough.'

He breathed heavily. 'It's being in this room. Look at all this,' he said. 'This bed, the table, the walls, the roof, floor, staircase. So much stuff. Masses of materials. And we don't need any of it. It's a great big waste. All we need is sand and stars above. A blanket.'

She shook her head. 'And the people we love.'

He saw her chin begin to wrinkle. His heart sank. He put an arm round her. She stiffened and squeezed her eyes and began to shake. 'I want to go home,' she wailed, in a voice all but shorn of consonants, then wept in earnest, hunching her shoulders tightly, as if hoping to stifle her sobs. He let her shake in his arms.

When the crying had passed it was as if the room had warmed up and the lamp's glow become golden. 'What a day,' he sighed. 'What a day.'

They lay back, arms beneath one another's necks.

'What a month,' she said. She turned to him. 'Just think. If you hadn't seen me in the hotel in Algiers.'

'If I hadn't decided to come down and get that drink.' He shook his head. 'And come and said hello. All because of a glass of pink milk.'

They lay in silence. The town was absolutely quiet outside.

'Seriously,' she said, turning half towards him. 'I have to go home. Really I do.'

Later, after she'd fallen asleep, he heard her moan in a dream.

The next day the consul arrived and the day after that they were in Casablanca. They sat in the lounge of a modern hotel drinking coffee. The hotel had a travel agency, and they were trying to resolve where to fly to. He had assumed she would come with him to London. She could meet the picture editors at the *Tribune*, and possibly they could fix up a regular contract for her. Sure enough, they had used several of her pictures, and one had been on the front page. They clearly liked her material. Then the two of them could be sent off together again.

'After something like that.' She shook her head. 'I don't know, I feel different. I need to stay at home for a while. Or at your flat in London.'

'I told you, I don't have one now.'

She frowned. 'Well, where would we stay?'

'I guess at a hotel for a few nights. Or with friends. Then wherever they send us next.'

He didn't like to see that she didn't know, or had forgotten, that he had no permanent home in London just now. It underscored what he hated to think of, that they had only known each other six weeks. He wanted it to be six months, six years. There was something indecent about it being so short a time.

She didn't reply. She was looking down at her coffee

cup, slowly stirring it. Then she laid the spoon in the saucer.

'This is crazy. Here we are about to get on a plane and we don't even know where we're going.'

'We're going to London.'

'I mean – next week, or the week after, or whatever. Where will we be?'

'Well, how would you want to do it?'

'Go home. And stay there as long as I need to. Sort my new pictures, send the best of them to the library. Maybe make a trip to Paris to see some friends, a couple of picture editors. And I'll have to get new cameras.' She paused. 'And see my family.'

She drank from her cup. 'Normally, well, a lot of my life, I have been trying to get away from them, and from France. But now I need to go.' She paused again. 'I nearly died,' she managed to say, before her bottom lip started trembling again. Then she sniffed, and pulled a smile. 'It's OK. You can come and join me. Or I'll come to London. It's OK, really. Then we'll wait till the next assignment.'

Even as she said the last words Mortimer could see a cloud pass over her face. He sank into dread. Was it that he didn't want to wait? He wanted no hiatuses now, but to keep on the move? So perhaps he could go to France with her. Idle a few weeks there, on her territory. That could be wonderful, possibly. Except he could imagine doing it for a few days, not a few weeks.

She shook her head. 'I don't know what to say. I just want to go home. And I don't want to make you come.' She screwed up her face in a silent request for sympathy, and he couldn't resist embracing her. It never occurred to him that she might have been asking if he'd contemplate settling in France with her.

So he found himself alone on the flight to London.

24

Back in the city he discovered that he himself was the subject of a piece about the growing troubles in the Maghreb. Apparently all the journalists in Algeria had been sent packing, and he had been one of the last to leave, if not the last.

What he didn't know until he went down to Kepple's office the day after he arrived was that Celeste had taken many pictures of him on his camel, wrapped in a headscarf, and the Sunday supplement was planning to use one of them. Later, a woman rang him at the friend's flat where he was staying, and asked him a lot of questions. He was feeling so baffled at the bustle of London, with its thousands upon thousands of houses, and streams of traffic, and everything so weightily overbuilt, that he found he could hardly think about the desert, and answered her questions barely aware of what he was saying. That Sunday there was a profile on him. The writer had got wind of the fact that around the office he had jokingly been called 'Mortimer of the Maghreb'. They gave half the page to the interview, half to the photograph of him on a camel. He folded up the paper as soon as he saw it, read only the headline and lead paragraph. It was altogether embarrassing.

Celeste had also taken a number of classic shots that ran in the paper, as well as the magazine, and Kepple used everything Mortimer could give him. His were the first and last eyewitness accounts of the Tuareg Revolt; the most romantic war of the half-century, people called it.

If it hadn't been for Celeste's shots, and for their both having been in the midst of it, and for the unusual circumstances under which they'd happened upon the insurrection, and for the protagonists' having been the tall and mysterious heroes of the desert, there would never have been so much interest. The coverage was out of all proportion to the story's importance. *Le Monde* and *Die Zeitung* went to town, with front-page photos and a series of pieces. They had staffers write up much of it but they couldn't avoid using Mortimer too, he was the one person who had been there, in the thick of it. *Paris-Match* did a photo-essay of Celeste's pictures, and they too used Mortimer for a short piece.

It was all better than he would ever have dared imagine.

Kepple called him into his office. There was something about being in that huge room, with the typewriters hissing and whirring, the keyboards pattering, the people moving about, the white plastic cups of coffee on the desks, the trails of smoke rising up all over the room, gathering in a pall under the lights – this was the hive where the big events of the world were processed. It reminded him that there were big events, large forces at work out in the world. This was where the broad stage of human drama was written up. It wasn't so much that this place offered a kind of excitement, as that it was big. It had room for him. Here one might gain perspective.

'Congratulations, you're staff,' was the first thing Kepple told him, in his little office walled with glass at one side of the big room. 'Bill called down yesterday. Give the man a salary for God's sake. His exact words. We'll have to think about where to send you next. Nicaragua's the obvious place.'

'Well, I might need –' Mortimer began.

'Of course. Have a breather. A few more days off, whatever. You wouldn't have to leave till next week. We'll organise everything.'

As Mortimer crossed the teeming room towards the exit, he felt a powerful exhilaration; or rather, simply power. A strong, calm feeling. Some current had got hold of him and was on his side, was carrying him. True, he was worried about Celeste just then as well: about the need to go and see her in France, to persuade her to come with him, be part of the destiny that was surely unfolding for them. But just then he couldn't conceive that things wouldn't work out. Everything was on his side.

Saskia had tried to make contact with him. She had left messages at the news desk, and at the flat where he was staying. She had also written a letter, saying she had read his material and he shouldn't hesitate to call her, should he want to.

That too seemed a confirmation of the tremendous goodwill that had strayed into his life.

'Let me cook you dinner,' she said on the telephone.

And he couldn't resist. He was curious, more than anything, to know how it would feel to see her, now that he had crossed an invisible barrier, a barrier he never really believed was there, until he found himself on the other side of it. It wasn't exactly called success; more luck. Some people got on the right side of luck, and now he was one of them. And it was all because of Celeste, of having found love.

When he walked through the door of their old home, in which she still lived, it felt perfectly safe, harmless. He could hardly remember how oppressive it had once seemed. She gave him a hug in the hallway, and that too felt familiar and unthreatening. Her body was slight against him, slighter than he remembered, and warm. Her face looked sleek and good. Perhaps she had lost a little weight, not that she had ever been overweight; or perhaps she was wearing a little make-up. A smile suffused her face, and he saw with pleasure that it was a smile of pride.

'You know, it's unheard of, this level of interest,' she said. 'You're a star, you really are. I always knew you would be.'

And it was true that it had been Saskia who a year and a half ago had egged him on and urged him to call a contact at the BBC, and who had been waiting for him in a pub on Charlotte Street after the interview. She had also sent him a telegram in Kirghizia the day his first report aired on the television.

Can't you do something badly? Love, Es.

'Es' meant 'S'. Saskia. She had always been rooting for him.

He had crunched up a strip of bacon at breakfast in that Kirghiz hotel with the telegram before him, and washed it down with foul, strong Kirghiz coffee, and felt the pleasure of having a woman back home cheering him on.

He didn't stay for dinner now but drank three glassses of wine. When he left she kissed him in the hallway, a lingering kiss. He had to extricate himself tactfully.

'Not a good idea,' he said.

She rested her forehead on his chest and shook her head.

25

Paris-Match wanted to send Celeste to Singapore.

'Come with me. Please. Just this once. I need you with me,' she implored him down the telephone. 'Please.'

But he couldn't. 'They want me in Nicaragua. Can't you come there instead? Let me talk to the *Tribune*.'

Which he did. But Kepple said: 'If the pair of you want to become stringers for us somewhere, we might be able to work something out. But you'd have to be freelance again. And in one place. We could perhaps use someone in Delhi. But I can't tell the picture desk to make her staff, or where to send her. It's none of my business.'

He went to see her in France, in Pau, and spent three days there. He met her mother, a crisp, brisk woman with a silver bun of hair, and an uncle, a car dealer from

Bordeaux who wore a well-cut suit of a shiny, soft, blue cloth Mortimer had never seen before. Even the sister with the four children was stylish, and slender. Mortimer felt dowdy and scruffy in his corduroy jacket.

Celeste was very happy to have him there. She was excited and animated, and took him to several bars and cafés, and up to a panoramic overlook a few miles above the town. It was a misty, cloudy day, the fir trees looking sombre among the rocks on the hillsides, and a river thickly hissing far below.

'You go,' she said, and hugged him. She felt warm and good against him. 'You go to Managua. It'll be OK. Really it will. It's right, of course it is. I'll come and join you as soon as I'm back from Asia. We'll see each other a lot, and soon. We'll work it out. Of course we will.'

But there was something in her insistence, and her vagueness, that unsettled him. They hadn't worked anything out.

Even many years later when he thought about it he still couldn't understand, or even just remember, how exactly it had all unravelled.

She had been supposed to fly out to Nicaragua to be with him when she returned from Singapore. But three weeks later, she still hadn't even left France for the Far East.

'What's going on?' he asked her from his Managua hotel.

'I don't know.' She hesitated. 'I just can't leave yet. I don't feel right about it.' He heard her sigh. 'I belong here.'

'But I thought you were going to go soon, then come here.'

There was a long silence.

She inhaled, then sighed again. '*C'est difficile.*'

After another pause she said: 'Something's changed. Really, I'm not going to run around the world any more. And when I come to Managua, what will I do? Maybe I'll sell some pictures. But I don't want to be doing this in five years' time. So I think I'd better stop now. This is my chance, when they all like my work and I can switch and do what I want.'

He felt winded. He could hardly believe what he was hearing. 'So when are you planning to see me?'

'Soon, soon,' she said.

Somehow he felt he ought to have seen this coming. But what was he supposed to do? Move to Pau and write for the local gazette?

He flew back to see her again, and this time it was palpably different. She was still happy to see him, she couldn't help that: her whole body lit up at his side, he could feel it. Yet she was reserved too. And somehow the visit ended up feeling ordinary, like seeing each other was something they could do or not do. What was there left to discover? In which case, had their whole love been founded on novelty, and nothing else? Novelty of location, story, work, and ultimately of each other? So as soon as they knew one another through and through, the process had run itself out?

Or was it merely beginning? The mists of honeymoon

had burned off now, and the real life together was starting? That was what he had wanted to believe.

But then he wondered: perhaps it had just been an exotic romance after all: an elaborate and exhilarating one, but still, no more than that. Otherwise, how was it that he could be away from her, and miss her, yes, think about her many times a day, yes, but still manage to get on with his work, and still feel that in the end if he had to make a choice between her and his work, work would win. Surely none of these things would have been possible if he were absolutely, deeply and necessarily in love with her. Surely you could trust love to make you, force you to do what you most needed.

Then there was the phone call when she wouldn't answer his question about his coming to visit again. Instead, she said she wanted to write to him. She faxed a letter to his hotel later that day.

That too he should have seen coming. She had been seeing an old friend, and it was complicated. She needed to resolve that first. But the good thing was that she'd been commissioned to do a book – her very own book – on the shepherds of the Ardèche. There'd be an exhibition too, in Toulouse. She was happy about that, although she did still miss him, and would always love him.

Always? He couldn't bear to read that, or to think what it meant.

He missed her too, in a horrible way. He'd go to bed at night feeling sick as he lay down alone, every cell of his body yearning for her.

Weeks before, in the desert, Celeste had once said to

him, 'It feels like you're driving a tractor over my heart,' after he had responded too casually to a question about what they'd do once they left the Sahara. 'Should we be thinking ahead?' And he, not realising the implication at the time, had answered, 'Let's not think ahead.' To which her response had been silence. A long enough silence that he'd looked up from the notebook he was reading through. She had had her back to him. There was something about her posture, cross-legged on the sand floor of their little mud house in the oasis, her shoulders hunched. 'What's up?' he asked. Then she said the line about the tractor. And he realised what she had been asking, and instead of feeling tired, fed up with the problem of coupling, with its endless capacity to derail one's plans and slow one's life, as he habitually had with Saskia, his heart melted. That was the right phrase for it. It was as if his midriff turned to warm liquid.

Now he knew what she had meant about the tractor. His insides felt as if they had been exposed to the air, his skin broken up.

So why didn't he jump on a plane and go and declare himself once more, and stay there if need be? Force the issue.

He didn't know. Somehow it seemed wrong. It seemed there was another way. Perhaps that way was work.

He steeled himself for work. He told himself there was only one way to go. You kept your arms sunk to the elbow in life so you never had a moment to look back, you were too busy with what was under your nose. And you kept moving. Two months in Nicaragua, a month in Chile, two weeks in Panama, then back across the world to the Solidarity Marches in Poland. Then back to Central America.

He had himself sent to Honduras with two passports so he could get in and out of Salvador and Nicaragua without either country knowing he visited the other. Six months in, he spent a weekend in Mexico City with a Mexican newsreader, a tall woman with freckles, curly hair and large eyes, charmed by his British accent, so she said. By the end of the weekend he was fighting to disguise the fact that he could not bear to be touched by her. It was nothing against her; but he felt something vital within himself slip away, drain out of him, pass like water from a sieve, and the only chance he had to preserve it was to be alone, quietly, in a room on his own. Or else to be hard at work, hot on a trail; or else just to be struggling to keep up with events, scribbling and rescribbling in his notebooks, dinging the bell of his typewriter with dependable regularity – ten dings per cigarette. At that rate he knew he was in business.

Meanwhile, in Algeria, although the Tuareg Revolt dwindled to nothing, the country was set on its doomed course to chaos.

1994

I

Eighteen years later, Mortimer returned to London from a Colombian earthquake, from a devastated city in the country's southern mountains, a colonial gem, a graph of white, grill-windowed Spanish houses now reduced to rubble with four or five figures' worth of bodies trapped under it – no one was yet sure how many had died. And even the dead had not got off unscathed: coffins in the cemetery had rammed the walls of the Catholic cubbyholes in which they were billeted, battering the masonry until they launched themselves into the street; one sarcophagus had even erupted from the living-room wall of a house built against the cemetery and landed on a family's dining table, splintering it, and causing an elderly grandmother to die of a heart attack, thus joining her deceased husband who had happened to be in the very casket. Mortimer returned from that scene of carnage and devastation, of dusty faces, bleached moustaches, ghostly figures wandering through the pall of dust that hung like mist over the shattered city, to his London desk to find the new editor waiting for him.

'No time to unpack, my friend. We need you in Algiers

yesterday. The city's exploding. We've got to get you in before they shut down again.'

'Can't go home for a change of clothes?' Mortimer tried.

'You're staying at the Hilton, they'll wash your clothes.'

It was spring, the almond trees along the avenues of Algiers were in blossom.

The first afternoon he took a taxi down to the old city. Was it him – he was jet-lagged, had been travelling for twenty-four hours straight – or had the country changed? It was close on two decades since he'd been here. He had not walked two blocks when he felt he simply could not be out here on his own, without a guide. Although only two men actually approached him, one asking if he was looking for a hotel, the other offering hashish, he felt like a sitting duck, a marked man waiting to be ripped off, or mugged, or worse. Every pair of eyes bored into his back as he passed. The cafés full of black-haired men who looked up from their games of cards, the vendors lining the narrow streets, the loafers every-where just standing about and watching – all of them checked him out. And he wasn't even in the medina yet, these were the narrow streets just outside it, its overflow, still wide enough for *petits taxis* and donkey carts to creep down.

He ducked into a relatively quiet café and took a table in the corner. The waiter was a silver-haired man in a black waistcoat, and Mortimer felt safer within the orbit of a man in some kind of uniform. But the waiter spent a long time eyeing him up from the zinc counter, with its trays of upturned glasses, before he came over and took his order. In the end Mortimer's mint tea took such a long time to arrive that he put twenty dinars on the table – far too much, he was sure – and was just about to leave without his tea, had already stood up and begun walking to the door, when he heard a clamour outside. Men were chanting, and loudly, and coming closer. In no time at all the chanting was very loud, and a column of men came briskly up the little street, causing all the vendors outside to pick up their boxes and trays and press themselves against the café windows, darkening further what was already a dark interior.

Mortimer went over to see what was going on. Just outside, a young man in a black leather jacket attempted to lift his tray of pastries from the ground, to save it from the tramping boots of the marchers. The first men stepped over it, then one put his foot on a corner and the tray jumped, scattering all its thin cakes into the dust.

The men came through thick and fast, five, six, seven abreast, shouting their chant, storming through the old town. The heart of the procession came by, a wooden litter carried on the shoulders of four men. Mortimer's eye fell on one of the pall-bearer's throats, its tendons flexing as he too shouted the song. The volume swelled as the litter passed. In it, laid on rushes, wrapped in a flag, recognisable for what it was by the little peak at the rear where the feet were, travelled a corpse.

Perhaps it was an everyday funeral. But there was something so angry in the air that it felt like a crowd intent on an enemy. It pressed on towards the medina, many more following the body than had preceded it. After the last of them, the chanting lingered a moment in the streets, then was gone.

Mortimer stood at the grimy café window as the normal sounds returned — of footfalls, the clack of checkers, the chatting of men's voices — and found he was clammy with sweat.

The waiter brought over the tea but Mortimer was already on his way out.

Without looking back he walked to the seafront, where he could find a taxi.

What had been the matter with him years ago, charmed by all this chaos, envy, poverty? Everywhere, he saw unscrupulous eyes intent on getting what they could from him. As he sank into the seat of a Mercedes *grand taxi*, still faintly redolent of its original leather, he thought, thank God for the Hilton. When they stopped at a sprawling mess of an intersection, with streets coming in from every angle, and no vehicles seeming to pay any attention to the rules of traffic, his heart jumped into his throat, and he glanced at the lock on his car door. It was only when he crossed the hotel's big marble lobby and heard the soft ding of the lift arriving for him that he began to feel safe again.

Up in his room he had a long hot shower, feeling uncommon gratitude for decent plumbing and sanitary-ware, for a private bathroom in a spacious room. Though he wished they had larger towels. He couldn't quite get one round his waist, and had to shuffle to the bed with one draped over his shoulders, holding the other round his thighs.

He lay on the bed listening to the hum of the air conditioning, while outside beyond the boulevard in front of the hotel the sky grew pale over the sea as evening approached.

In a while he lifted the bedside receiver from its cradle.

The double ring tones of the English phone were restful and pleasing in the ear, reminders of a world of order and good sense, a world in which one could relax, breathe more easily. It occurred to him to wonder, as he lay there with the earpiece beside him on the pillow, what it was about that world of the old Arab town that seemed so forbidding, so foreign and so much like an enemy terri-tory. He had just been in Colombia, surely no less foreign, if anything more hazardous. Yet there he had not once felt so out of place. Or was there really a surge of anti-Western sentiment roiling about the narrow streets? This whole region, so different from the regulated and calm one he could hear declaring itself with its tidy, soft double alarums at the far end of the phone line, seemed endem-ically warlike and hostile, not just to outsiders but even to its own. Every town had its old ksar, its fortress. This had always been a land where to stray from your allotted terrain was to err into enemy territory.

But then, where on earth would that not be true of?

Perhaps he was getting too old for the field, too jumpy.

'Greetings from the Maghreb,' he said, and forced a chuckle. 'How are you?'

He heard her sigh. Her first utterance to him. His wife: Saskia.

He had been away ten days in the Andes, then been sent straight on to Algiers without even collecting a change of clothes, and all she could manage was a sigh.

He swallowed his irritation.

'Mrs Levinson had a go at me,' she said.

Mrs Levinson? He racked his brains and remembered: one of the boy's teachers. 'Really?' was all he could manage.

'She called me at work. I shouldn't have let Johnny go to school with that cough, can you believe it? He's thirteen. I had the Nigerian attaché on the other line. Anyway,' she checked herself. 'How are you?'

But she asked the question as a formality, with no trace of interest at all.

'OK, OK,' he said rapidly, to get off a subject that held no interest for her. 'Relieved to be in a decent hotel.'

For the first time, it crossed his mind she might not be happy that he was back in Algeria.

'It's mayhem here,' he said, hoping to dispel any notion of this being a trip down memory lane.

'That's what we've been hearing.' By 'we' she meant the aid agency for which she worked, Food International.

There was a pause. Then she said, 'Actually, I wanted to ask. You couldn't swing a trip to the south while you're there? There are a hundred thousand Malian refugees in southern Algeria. It should be in the nationals.'

'Can you fax me something?' he said, reverting to professional ground. 'Hold on.' And he got up to fetch the fat fake-leather folder of hotel information.

When he got back she too said, 'Hold on,' and went to find paper and pen.

Outside the window, a pool of opal sky was being swamped by a bank of cloud darker than smoke, so that it seemed like night itself coming in. He felt all the more reassured to be in a comfortable modern hotel room far above the teeming city, lying in the glow of three pairs of fake gilt carriage lamps.

2

Mortimer's career had gone from strength to strength. Back in 1978 the paper had changed his contract and put him on a megalith of a retainer, as Kepple called it, and made him their 'World Correspondent'. Ever since he did a Latin American series for the *Washington Post* — reluctantly the *Tribune* had assented, there being nothing in his contract about transatlantic exclusivity — that won him a Pulitzer, other papers had opened the door to him. Chronicler of wars and ruptured governments, interviewer of popes and pashas, he had had columns set aside for him in papers the world over. He had interviewed Reagan over a dinner of Maine lobster, and Castro over Cohibas and *mojitos*. It was true that on both these occasions other journalists had been present, and they had been publicity stunts, but still, it was something to tell the grandchildren. Or would have been had there been any. He had drunk beer with the mad Billy Fuentes, beer baron of Bolivia, commanding chief of the death squads. He had been the toast of London and Washington. Mother Teresa and the Dalai Lama had agreed to a joint interview with him. Noriega himself had bestowed the Order of the Silver Pelican on him, and the Queens of Norway and Tonga had awarded him honorary degrees. For eighteen years Mortimer had ridden the biggest waves in the business. Embracer of causes, instigator of hunts, winner of media coups, Mortimer had redefined his profession.

Several times over the years he had nearly got back in touch with Celeste. He had meant to, planned to, decided to, even written letters. But then thought he should rewrite parts of them, and kept intending to, but put it off until gradually the impulse would sink away and the weeks became months, and finally years.

He and Saskia had staged their recovery two years after he'd been in the desert. He was sent down to Conakry, Guinea, in West Africa, where the iron-fisted dictator Sekou Toure had decided to crack open the tight seal he kept on his country, and allow in a little foreign invest-ment. The whim hadn't lasted – he didn't like to share – and he'd soon slammed the door shut again. But it so happened that Saskia too was sent down by her aid agency at the same time. A lot of aid people had come down. The two of them had had a fling, then more. Afterwards, every time he came through London he saw her. And her child: she had a young son, by an American diplomat who had run out on her, who in fact already had a family.

He'd walk or take a taxi down the old street where they had once lived together, and feel a growing, calm pleasure to be back. He'd remember their old joke when

he saw the doorbell that said 'Press' on its white ceramic.
'Press? I'm press.'

Eventually they had married. They had done it quietly
in the registry office – quietly, that is, until the boy started
whining, then bawling when she strapped him in his
pushchair.

Mortimer had found it hard to adjust to life with a
toddler; or rather, the Western way of living with one.
The cot, the pushchair, the large toys – there seemed so
much paraphernalia, all of it designed to keep the child
away from its mother. The net result was a screaming
child. He couldn't help noticing that in the Third World,
where children were not religiously put to bed at seven
o'clock on their own, the babies seemed never to cry.
They lived on their mother's backs.

He found himself disagreeing, even disapproving of
Saskia's way of doing things. Yet it was none of his business, not just because she didn't want it to be, nor because
the child wasn't his, but because he came and went so
much. When the child had croup it had been Saskia's
mother who was around, who had come to stay for three
weeks. Mortimer had been in Mozambique, then was sent
directly to Sri Lanka. Sometimes he got the feeling the
household ran more smoothly, and that Saskia was happier,
when he was gone. For months on end she seemed to
have little for him except impatience and annoyance. And
she became ever less guarded about showing it.

He knew he was a dismal kind of partner. But he
couldn't see what he could do to become better, short
of changing his profession. He made a point of bringing

back gifts from every trip – some local toy or costume from the market for Johnny, once he discovered how much the boy enjoyed dressing up, and for her a cosmetic he knew she used from duty-free, and a rug, a sculpture, a small painting. Fortunately she liked ethnic art. Though whenever he strayed into ethnic dress of any kind, whatever it was would vanish into the wardrobe never to emerge again.

Sometimes it was lovely to come home – the boy eager to see him and get his present, which over the years moved into duty-free electronics, and Saskia welcoming him with a smile and a joyous time in bed, where it would be both warmly familiar and exhilarating after the abstinence. But more often he would have the sense he had walked in on some troublesome scene that his presence would only make worse. And on top of that, though their sex life had never been explosive, after the blow of a child, it had never recovered. Sometimes when he was home he felt like an interloper, an unwanted guest; anything but the returning champion that just occasionally he'd have liked to fancy himself. It seemed that any good feeling he managed to rouse through his professional endeavours he could count on her to crush.

Now and then they'd get a babysitter and he'd take her out to dinner, and she'd dress up a little, and a shine of affection, or better, would return to her eyes.

Most often when they went out it was to dinners, functions, parties that one way or another had a bearing on his professional life. She would accompany him when she could, being ever on the lookout for funds and exposure for her agency. But it was a sadness to him that she seemed to have lost any pride she had ever had in the accomplishments of her partner. Sometimes he even wondered if she wasn't somehow resentful of them – as if given more freedom, more encouragement, she could have done the same; even, occasionally, as if she were actually envious. It wasn't always pleasant to climb into bed beside her.

But then he could always draw comfort from his work: he knew he could not have asked for a career that had gone better.

3

Lying in his hotel room now, in Algiers again after so many years, drying off on the warm, damp towels spread over the bed, and experiencing just a little prick of a chill, which prompted him to pull on his trousers then resume his position, he gazed at what he could see of his reflection hovering in the dark glass against the blackness of the Mediterranean night: pale brown slacks, the white bulk of the torso, the high ruddy forehead, a forehead that now more or less reached all the way back to the crown of the head. He hadn't shaved lately – he would often stop while away – and just now had a short grizzled beard.

It wasn't the look of his expanded body but something else that unsettled him. He became inexplicably restless, with an uncomfortable constriction in his chest. He decided to dress and go down to the bar.

★   ★   ★

The Hilton bar was crawling with journalists. A bearded young man from *Paris-Match* who Mortimer had met a couple of times before offered him a beer, then asked if he'd like to ride with him the next day in the Mercedes the magazine had hired for him. He wanted Mortimer to drive so he could shoot from the car window. 'You know the city,' he added.

'It's been a long time,' Mortimer said. But he was happy to oblige. It would save him having to rely on taxis.

Then he ran into two old acquaintances he'd once worked with years ago in television.

'That wouldn't be Mortimer of the Maghreb?' a gravelly voice asked. It was Harry, a news producer at the BBC. 'You've had a few meals since I last saw you.' He spluttered an alcoholic laugh.

Mortimer patted his belly. 'Best part of the job, the varied cuisine. You haven't changed at all.'

It was true. Harry still had the same red, ageless face, a bit less hair and a few more wrinkles, but Mortimer would have recognised him at once. Not so his sidekick Jimmy, though, the cameraman, who had lost most of his hair and whose face had reddened to the same hue as his boss's. He sported a pair of thick, ginger sideburns now.

'You two aren't still working together?'

'Why not?' Jimmy asked.

'If you can call it work,' Harry growled. 'It's not like it used to be. Christ, never mind you, soon even we'll be out of a job.'

Mortimer had worked with the two of them on his very first television stories.

'These days,' Harry went on, 'all you need is some film student with a video camera, you hook them up to a satellite antenna, and away you go. There's no skill left. Just point and shoot.'

'What are you talking about, Harry? Let me buy you a drink.'

Harry swirled his whisky glass, drained it, then set it down. 'Reporting as you and I know it is over. The punters want to see it as it happens. Don't tell me you hadn't noticed.'

'I hadn't noticed.'

'History unfolding before their eyes, type thing,' Jimmy added.

Mortimer shrugged. 'News can't go out of style. It's the nature of the beast. What'll it be, whiskies all round?'

'Our kind of news can. Cheers. On the spot, live feed, it's the way everyone's going. Anyway, what the devil have you been up to? Apart from eating.'

'I take it you don't read the papers,' Mortimer replied.

'Not if I can help it. They're all junk too these days. Columns and whatnot.'

'Well, here's to old times,' Mortimer said.

Later, they had a well-lubricated dinner of couscous and kebabs.

4

The next morning, in a dazzle of hangover, Mortimer drove through a bright spring day towards the convulsing centre of the city, with the French photographer beside him in the passenger seat. They headed straight for the medina.

Had he been alone, would he have done anything differently? Sometimes he liked to think so. It hadn't helped that the car had been that gleaming Mercedes, of all things, a symbol of Western power, Western carelessness.

When they stopped at a junction Mortimer said, 'Last time I was down here it was also with a *Paris-Match* photographer. Celeste Dumas.'

The man smiled and nodded. 'Sure. She's a great photographer. She moved on from journalism. She's done well for herself. You can't go into a poster shop in France without finding one of her pictures. Shepherds, peasant farmers, goats and mountains, that kind of thing. She's good.'

Mortimer crept across the intersection, and up a smaller street away from the sea.

'Do you know her?'

'I've met her.'

'She and I, we went right down into the desert,' he said, driving slowly up the street.

'I'd love to do that,' the man said softly. 'One day when it's safe again.'

They hadn't yet reached the medina, just the narrow streets near it, when they hit trouble: shouts echoed among the buildings, then they reached a corner and heard the roar of a mob. Halfway down the block they saw them, youths shouting as they ran down a cross-street, carrying things. Mortimer couldn't make out what they held, in the brief moment before he looked back over his shoulder to reverse the car, but he had the unmistakable impression that most of them had objects in their hands.

He couldn't tell if it was the commotion in the streets, or hearing about Celeste, but something had disturbed him. He had that same constriction in the chest again, and felt impatient, irritable.

They cruised around, trying to gauge where the heart of the action was, and how to approach it, and how closely, when a column of protesters rounded the corner into a street they were crawling down. Mortimer at once turned the car, a five-point turn, cursing himself for not simply having reversed, only to find another brisk phalanx filing along the next cross-street, blocking their exit.

There was nothing for it. He drove slowly towards the column. Only when the car was twenty yards off did it attract the attention of the crowd. A crop-headed young man seemed to smile at Mortimer, pointed and shouted. Then three or four youths, perhaps students, Mortimer thought, filtered away from the main procession, jogging towards the car. For a moment Mortimer thought they had gone right past, their attention on something else, until a sharp, loud knock on the roof made him bounce in his seat.

'*Vas-y, vas-y,*' shouted the Frenchman beside him.

How to drive through a crowd: there was a proper speed for it, just fast enough to show that you meant to keep going, slow enough to let them get out of the way. Which they did. They paused, waited for the car to pass, and Mortimer drove through. Perhaps most of the crowd hadn't yet realised that this vehicle was legitimate prey, at least as far as the radicals were concerned. But the youths were still shouting, and someone caught on and gave the roof another slap, loud enough that Mortimer thought it must have been delivered with a hard object.

'*Dieu, Dieu,*' the Frenchman said, looking round as they drove away. He shook his head. 'Do you know how lucky that was?'

'What do you think? Park and keep out of the way?'

'Not here,' the Frenchman exclaimed.

They crawled down the street away from the medina, passing a group of three photographers who were jogging down a block. Mortimer slowed and offered them a ride but they all declined. Then they ran into an angrier, faster crowd, a mob further down the road to violence. They appeared behind the car, rounding the nearest corner.

Mortimer looked back over his shoulder. The crowd were shaking their fists, ululating, slapping their wrists in some local gesture, and filled the narrow street. The odd stone and bottle flew towards the car, nothing too serious. If the rioters had really wanted to damage the vehicle, Mortimer sensed they could have done a lot worse. But there was no telling what might come next. Perhaps they knew now who was in the car, and wanted the foreign journalists out. The very presence of the Western media would be emblematic of everything the Islamists despised about the current government, with its readiness to get in league with the profane might of the West.

He wasn't taking any chances, and started to drive while still looking back, watching the crowd behind. Someone started running after the car, drawing back their arm to launch some kind of missile. Mortimer put his foot down, and turned forwards just in time to see a man clad in a white jellaba and a grey, wool skullcap launch himself into the road. At first Mortimer thought the man must have been pushed, or lost his step. The Frenchman screamed, 'Watch out!' Mortimer saw the man's face, screaming too, the cropped white beard, brown teeth, sparkling eyes, creased cheeks. He jabbed the brakes and swerved but too late. A double knock came, first an axle-jarring jolt, then a thud as the forehead delved into the windscreen.

Mortimer stopped and began to open his door, but the Frenchman shouted, '*Non, non*. Go!'

He looked back and saw a lot of people running at the car.

'Go, go!' shouted the Frenchman again.

Without thinking, he closed his door and accelerated, felt the car break free, lurch forwards as if suddenly lighter, as the man slid off the bonnet. The last thing to go was his hand, apparently attempting to clutch at the windscreen. The car bumped over something in the road.

The one good thing was that the glass didn't shatter. Or perhaps it would have been better if it had. Mortimer would then have had to stop. But there was only a misty web of splinters where the head had hit. Mortimer heard a lot of shouting close by, just outside the car, and above the roar of the mob behind, the whine of the powerful, well-tuned engine was inaudible.

At the first corner the tyres squealed on the smooth cobbles as he made the turn. The big car travelled slowly round the bend. Something made Mortimer glance out of his window. He found himself staring straight into the large blue eye of a camera lens. A bald-headed man with a video camera on his shoulder was stooping to get the shot of the car's driver.

Mortimer looked back in amazement, for just long enough to see the cameraman train his lens on the car a moment as it drove away, then lift his contraption off his shoulder and proceed to run down the street, away from the advancing mob. Mortimer's startled face must have been the last thing he shot, before the riot exploded all through the streets of central Algiers, and the foreign journalists had either to flee the country or go into hiding.

'Bloody hell,' Mortimer said. 'Did you see that? He was filming us.'

Mortimer had seen cameramen get like that before. Once in Sri Lanka he'd watched a tall Argentinian wait until an angry crowd had closed around him, until he stood with his machine by his head like a rock rising above a tide. He'd got lucky, that Argentinian, the mob had had other things on their mind. All the journalists saw him later at the bar of the hotel they were staying in. There hadn't been the backslapping and rowdy toasting one might have expected. Rather, people kept their distance, talked in lowered voices. Partly, it was jealousy: that man would have the best footage, no question. But also theirs could be a dangerous game. With every new risk some hot-blooded hack took, the danger rose for all of them.

The Frenchman pointed ahead. 'There's the future.'

Halfway down the block a large white Mazda van was parked at the kerb. It had a telescopic hoist on its roof with a satellite dish at the top. The dish was tipped at the sky, the point of its silver antenna beaming into space.

Mortimer didn't recognise that the bald cameraman had been Jimmy until he saw, in the window of the van, Harry the producer's face. Their eyes met. Mortimer lurched with a shock of recognition.

'Bloody hell.'

'Live feed,' the Frenchman said. 'They watch it back in Lyons as it happens. Our game is over.'

'Balls,' Mortimer said, accelerating down to the boulevard that ran along the foot of Algiers' hills. 'Video was supposed to kill the cinema.' He shook his head. 'What did that idiot think he was doing, jumping a moving car?'

'They don't think.'

'They could use us, we're not the enemy.'

They sped east towards the Hilton.

'Was it bad?' Mortimer asked. 'Did it look bad?'

The Frenchman shrugged. '*Pas tellement*. But that's not so good,' he said, nodding towards the shattered dent in the windscreen.

The Algerian's grey cap had attached itself to one of the wipers. 'Get rid of it,' the Frenchman snapped. Mortimer switched on the wipers. The cloth hat waved back and forth, clinging to a join in the blade's mechanism as the rubber scraped over the broken glass.

The car cruised rapidly along the avenue, the shadows of the blossom-covered trees flicking over it.

1997

I

Mortimer was in a taxi again, he was forever in taxis these days, and never did he seem to have to pay for them. He'd reach into his wallet not quite sure what he'd find, certainly a few crumpled ones, a five, with any luck a twenty or two, though he'd be preferring to hold on to those just a little longer, you never knew when they might be called on for a tumbler or two of the Finest Ballantines.

He got out at his local, on Seventh Avenue, and pressed into its welcome dark. Five thirty: he was a little early.

It was OK to live as he was, in one long ragged celebration, or commiseration, as long as one had a target, a destination, a point at which one could get off because one had to, in order to return necessarily to the desk and the keyboard. But for many months now he had not had that. Years. It had been Clive, an old friend and colleague from the *Tribune*'s features page, now 'Consulting Editor' for a glossy, who had got him over to New York as a 'Roving Editor', whatever that was. He had organised the visa, the sub-let, the modest but decent retainer, which ought to have been enough to cover his basic costs but wasn't. The idea had been that on top, he would receive a generous fee per story.

So far it hadn't worked out. What was to have been his first story, on the Drugs War in Colombia – 'A war of sorts,' Clive said – was pulled from Mortimer's fingers and given to some young blood from Atlanta.

That had been four months ago now. Just this afternoon there had been a message on Mortimer's phone machine from Clive about another possible story he'd been hoping for: 'I'm sorry, Charlie,' it said, 'that story isn't going to work out after all. Can we get together tomorrow or something? Give me a call?'

Mortimer suspected what it meant: he had been in New York for months and still not a single story: his retainer couldn't go on for ever. Clive had gone out on a limb for him.

Yet why hadn't things worked out? He was as good as he had ever been. It seemed it had nothing to do with his skills, and everything to do with luck. Or not luck exactly, but having the world on your side. When he had started out as a young man, he had loved the world; then he had felt the world start to love him. And look where it all ended up.

When Clive had first called him in London and offered the position, Mortimer had leapt at the chance to get away. It had seemed that at last he might escape the swamp his life in London had become. It wasn't *his* life any more. It was someone else's, and somehow he had mistakenly been transplanted into it. This other person wrote nothing but reviews of restaurants, and of stray fashions that swept through the capital. They didn't travel at all, ever, except for the cab rides that trundled them to their many meals. They drank wine ceaselessly. And when they weren't drinking wine they drank whisky with a little water. They didn't like many things. They tended to thunder at the keyboard complaining about whatever struck them as new and unnecessary.

Fads and food: these were his subjects now. What they wanted was a cantankerous old colonel, and that was what they got: a sodden old colonel of the press, retired from the field.

'At least you've got the build for it,' an old colleague remarked when he heard Mortimer was doing restaurant reviews these days.

'I've had a bit of training,' Mortimer conceded.

The rushed and meaningless columns for the *Standard* would feel already soggy with the next day's fish-and-chips even as he banged them out. He wasn't sure what to call it but something unpleasant made its home in him; despair, or loneliness, or chaos. Its effect was to hurl him headlong down the face of a wave with a churn of anxiety and fury in his belly.

Nor could he believe how fast time was flying these days. It was in fact three whole years since his great mistake in Algiers; it still felt like three weeks. He kept waiting to be sent back to the pine-clad valleys and dusty cities where a man like him belonged, and couldn't understand why it wasn't happening.

Eighteen months back Saskia had finally left him. Which was to say: thrown him out. He had come home drunk one morning with what looked like an egg stain down one lapel, to find his bags literally packed for him in the hall. He had stared at them and thought, 'Hello? A trip somewhere?'

The note was on the kitchen table: *I can't bear this any longer. Please don't be here when I get back.*

Even then, seeing his sentence of banishment, he had felt not dread or guilt, but curiosity. At least this was something *new.*

Three years ago, after the Algiers accident, the hacks had had a field day with him.

'Once dubbed Mortimer of the Maghreb by his colleagues, British journalist Charles Mortimer is at the centre of an international controversy over the role of Western news reporting.'

The BBC. *The Nine O'Clock News.* Fourth story up, with the damning footage from Algiers played in slow motion.

It was the video age. Within seven minutes the images had been in Atlanta, all over the world. Jimmy, planted by fate on that street corner in Algiers, had been filming live. It was golden stuff for him: a dramatic scene from a country in collapse, a car knocking a man flying, then a long, slow close-up of the driver, apparently showing no remorse, no inclination to halt the hit-and-run. And of all people it had been the distinguished reporter.

The footage was syndicated across America that night, and the BBC aired it right away. There his face was, the jowls grizzled with a few days' growth, the wild spray of hair well past due for a cut around the expanded fore-head, the broad, mottled nose, and the startled, grey eyes.

'Can we trust our reporters?'

It was the worst it could be. It had been the beginning of the end. Thereafter, he was no longer a war reporter, a true journalist. After all, what real news was there bar wars?

It was the *Standard* who came along and offered him a column. 'Can't bear to see a good man go to waste,' the woman said. She offered to put him to work writing about restaurants. 'Are you serious?' he asked. Then told himself: I'm a professional, if they want arugula and Montepulciano, that's what I'll give them.

The bad luck hadn't been the Frenchman insisting they speed on, nor the car being a Mercedes, a sleek symbol of Western mercantile imperialism; nor the reckless, brain-fevered fundamentalist deciding to attack bare-handed a speeding vehicle with its freight of infidel media. It had been Jimmy the cameraman valiantly staying his ground to squeeze in a few more seconds of footage.

He knew he had made a mess of things. That wasn't the problem. That could one day be addressed, fixed, forgiven. The problem, which knew no solution, was to have made a mess of himself.

2

A few months after the debacle, he had received a letter from Celeste. She'd sent it care of the old paper, who had forwarded it.

What a lot of asses they are. Anything to get their names out there. To make things seem important when they aren't. Anyway, I was glad to hear news of you at last, even bad news. I've read your stuff now and then. It has been so long. Again and again I have wanted to know what has happened to you, but also been scared to know, I don't know why. Have you ever wondered about me? It brought it all back, hearing of you, seeing your face. I hope it is all right for me to write to you. Surely it is. We are adults. You can't imagine how I missed you. Often I used to think our timing was wrong but everything else was right. I have no regrets in life except you.

Let me know if you're ever in Paris, I'll come and see you. But don't worry. Just if you can, if you'd like.

Thinking of you, Celeste.

The letter also told him that she had two teenage daughters, her husband Eric was a psychiatrist at a local hospital, and they lived, along with two donkeys, a few goats and a lot of geese, in an old farmhouse she had restored in the Ardèche. She hoped he got through this nonsense quickly, and didn't let it bother him.

It bothered him for a start that even in France they had evidently heard about his downfall. But that was only the start of it. That letter had been just what he didn't need.

He did go to France, and he oughtn't to have done. He went shamefaced, hangdog, pretending to himself that he had been planning to go to Paris anyway in order to review – or rather to demolish – a trendy new eatery whose young owner, a rock-star chef as he called him, had been charming the journalists of half the European papers. The *Standard* agreed to send him over a few weeks after he received Celeste's letter, and he wrote back to the address she had given telling her where he'd be staying.

She called him three days later.

The strange thing was that the sound of her voice, far from alarming him as he'd expected, or plunging him into old feelings of guilt or panic, or making him worry further about what a mess he seemed to have made of his life, simply made him smile. Once or twice in the years after they split up they had had a little sporadic contact, but it must have been twelve years, he thought, if not fifteen, since he had actually heard that soft, breathy yet musical timbre of hers in his ear.

'*Bonjour*,' she said, with a playful lilt. She was clearly happy to be speaking to him. At once – in the face of everything that had been going on, the collapse of his true career, his public disgrace, the growing resentment Saskia bore him – at once an unexpected joy welled up in him. And he found himself smiling, telephone in hand.

'How are you holding up?' she asked.

He could tell that she too was smiling.

'Much better this morning,' he declared. 'It's damn good to hear your voice.'

She chuckled. 'Me too,' she said, in a little confusion. 'I mean, it's good to hear yours too.'

It was such a light-hearted experience, that phone call, that it seemed easy and natural that they agree to meet the following week, when he would be in Paris. The only problem, she said, was that it would be hard for her to get to Paris after all, as one of her kids had exams, but would he like to come and visit. The new train could get him there in two hours, and they had plenty of room.

He hesitated a moment.

She said: 'Eric would love to meet you. And actually he is very busy that week, we will have plenty of time to talk, to catch up.'

And he thought to himself: the war is over, all campaigns are dead, this is not about a long-lost romance into which new life may be breathed. This is about restoration, recovery, the need to get a little perspective. The long view: that's what's required at such a time, and that's what she's offering. So he went.

When he stepped off the train on to the platform, where only one other person, an elderly woman, disembarked, he had the sense that he physically felt her at the end of the station wall before he actually saw her. She was standing there in a camel coat, a scarf round her neck, and her arms crossed. He walked towards her, and had the unnerving sensation that the platform had developed a gelatinous surface, that he couldn't trust each footfall not to squirm about and upset his stride. Then for a moment it was as if his soles didn't even quite make contact with the ground, but hovered on an uncertain cushion of air.

It was a cloudy morning, and it had been raining. The very air seemed impregnated with grey. The trees beyond the station were black, and the tarmac of the car park outside shone.

Celeste was much darker than he remembered. Her face had a rich, nutty tan. But the eyes were exactly the same, and so were the bones under the skin, the shape of her face. He registered that she had more wrinkles, especially around the eyes, and her dimples had deepened, but he did not exactly see these things. He saw straight through them to her real face, the face that no amount of time could change.

They embraced, and he noticed how warm her body felt, in spite of the chilly day. Or perhaps because of it. And her cheek against his, as they briefly kissed each other, was somehow simultaneously both hot and cold, as if a chill lay on the surface of her skin, but beneath it her face was warm. It was surprising, and somehow wonderful, to notice these things.

She said that she had a bottle of wine in the car – a big Citroën estate car – and thought they might drive to a scenic spot and raise a glass to old times. He thought he detected a nervousness, or a guardedness in her, and promptly agreed. He added: 'That sounds great.'

But he wondered if after all she didn't want him in her home, and perhaps had not even mentioned his visit to her husband. Or maybe after their drink she would take him to their house.

He slung his overnight bag in the back of the car and they sat in silence a while as she steered out of the station, then out of the small town on to a smooth new road that wound down the valley they were in.

'Well, thank you for seeing me,' he said.

'Thank you for coming.' He saw her smile in profile.

She glanced at him and they both laughed. She put her hand on his knee for a second. 'It's nice to see you.'

'You too,' he said, then felt a little foolish, as if he had said something quite unnecessary.

After another pause they both began to speak at the same time, and stopped, and laughed again. Then they both waited for the other to talk first, and neither said anything.

'You first,' he said after a moment.

'No, you.'

And again they laughed.

'So how are you?' he said finally.

And the question seemed embarrassingly lame, and somehow formal, after all that preamble.

Finally they turned on to a lay-by high up a valley-side, then drove down a track through a pine wood for quarter of a mile, and parked in a clearing. There was a narrow deep gorge at the end of the little space, and you could hear the thunderous roar of a river a hundred feet below. A metal bench had been erected near the ravine, and Celeste had thought to bring a sheet of plastic to put on it, along with the bottle of red wine and two paper cups. She had opened the cork earlier and shoved it halfway back in the neck.

'It's funny,' she said, once they were seated, 'all this recent stuff that happened to you in Algiers. I mean, it's not funny at all, it's terrible. But that it should have been in Algeria. I think it's that that brought everything back to me. Made me feel I had to get in touch. I hope you don't mind.'

He responded automatically that of course he didn't mind, and then noticed that far from not minding, he was delighted. He couldn't have explained how or why, but to be sitting here with her in this improbable place – having just stepped off a train, on a dreary day in the small mountains of south-central France – felt like the most natural thing in the world. He even had a curious sense of something he could only call belonging. As if all the problems, efforts and striving that his life ordinarily seemed to consist of – and the boredoms and irritations – had all quite naturally abated, because at last, however unwittingly, he had won through to where he belonged.

This is ridiculous, he told himself; but it is nice too, so I don't mind. And even that – the capacity to accept the situation and how it felt, along with its implausibility – even that felt like a curious blessing he was being granted.

They raised their glasses and looked at each other, and Celeste held his gaze with her eyes that were green and blue, and also flecked with rust, with straw, with what looked like gold in the sombre daylight in the woods.

'So,' she said. 'This is crazy. Me dragging you down here.'

'You didn't drag me.'

She sighed. 'I feel I want to tell you about my life, tell you everything, but I don't know where to begin.'

'You're a big success.'

'What about you? Look at you. But that's not what I mean. I mean, what happened to us, and what happened after.'

There was something about the way she said it. It wasn't just the implicit certainty or conviction that whatever they'd shared had been important; it was more than that, she accepted it as a God-given and obvious fact that it had been a major thing. So much so that without even checking with him, she went on: 'Sometimes really I don't know if I ever got over it. Sometimes I used to curse and curse myself for not going with you. To Nicaragua. And even this, to see you now, this is a great privilege. I mean, I have had a good life. Touch wood, so far. I love my husband and my children, and my home, my work. I have friends all over, all over France. I sell my pictures, everything is good, it's not just some shallow, petit-bourgeois life, it's a good life. Good. Eric is a good man, a tender, sensitive, intelligent man. And helpful. We can talk about almost anything. We laugh a lot.' She nodded to herself and frowned slightly. 'We love each other.' She chuckled. 'Maybe I sound like I'm trying to convince myself but I'm not, it really is good, and enriching, fulfilling, all of that. But you and me. We never finished. I think that's what it is, or was, a sense of incompleteness. It took a long time for that to fade in me. That feeling. And for years and years sometimes it would come back. Why didn't I go with you? Was I right that I needed to settle down? And now all this stuff that has been going on with you, in the newspapers, on the television and radio, and it all happening in Algeria, where we were. I'm sorry, I just thought, now I must see him. It is late enough. My elder daughter is doing her *baccalauréat*, Ondine the younger one will do hers in two years. They are nearly grown up. And maybe, well, you must be suffering now, this cannot be easy, all this nonsense, and I thought maybe, just maybe I can help you somehow. Especially with our link with Algiers. All of that. I'm sorry, I'm telling you all this, but I don't know how long we have, and when we will see each other again, there is no time for formalities. Can it be a bad idea? How can it be a bad idea? How can it?'

She fell silent and looked at him a moment. As soon as she looked away he felt that he had been wearing a smile on his face all through her speech: a mix of surprise, of pleasure and something like wonder had called the smile forth. The lightness of his heart had grown and grown until his heart was just about ready to float into the sky. It was a sensation he hadn't known in decades.

But she looked away now, down into the ravine. He glanced at the side of her face, and wondered if he ought to have been smiling after all. He could still hear her question: how can it be a bad idea? She meant to see him, of course. Could he reach out and take her hand? That was what he wanted to do, what perhaps also he ought to do. But just as he was deliberating, he saw a mottling of tiny wrinkles appear on her chin. Then her shoulders hunched silently, and she shook a little, and a full tear ran swiftly down her cheek, undulating a little over the minor folds of her skin. He watched the tear make its track, and another that welled over her nearer eyelid to follow it, and the strange thought came to him: those tears are what happened to my life. He had no idea why the thought should be there, or what exactly it meant, but somehow it seemed to fit with this strange day, to be of a piece with this implausible rendezvous.

She began to shake her head gently as she wept. He put his arm round her, and she let him, but equally she did not respond to it. He felt her cold now, stiff within his embrace. He sat there holding her, letting her cry. He didn't understand why she was crying; at least he didn't feel like crying himself, but he felt something very serious was going on; something serious for him, as well as for her. In a curious way, he didn't feel that he had to understand just what it was. That part didn't seem so important: it mattered more just that this be happening.

Then on an impulse he squeezed her hand and leaned close and kissed her wet cheek. He kept his lips there, and held her tight, and mumbled, 'It's OK, it's OK,' repeatedly. Even that he didn't really know why he was saying, but it felt true, and right.

When he thought back to this moment later, he realised that one remarkable thing about it had been that in spite of being presented with this copious volume of feeling from her, he had not felt in the slightest bit alarmed. He had just wanted to be there with her through her suffering.

And it had turned out to be quite brief. After a while she shrugged and wiped the back of a hand over her face, then rummaged first in one pocket then the other, found a tissue to wipe her cheeks with, and blew her nose noisily. Then she let out a kind of laugh that was also a sigh. He touched her cheek with his hand. After all these years he felt that he could. And apparently he could. She smiled, and leaned her face against his palm.

That, for him, was the fatal moment. The years seemed to crumple. It was as if you folded a piece of paper so the two furthest edges came together. Two decades were swallowed up in a moment. They didn't vanish; they simply had never been. It was suddenly abundantly plain that nothing of any importance whatsoever in his life had happened between this day and the last time he saw Celeste. The whole intervening period had been so insignificant that some part of his brain – or worse than that, some universal law or other – had simply not acknowledged those years at all. They were just chaff, and rightly blew away in the wind. And this, here in his hand now, was the grain: the only thing that mattered at all.

He had the strange sense that even this experience with Celeste, begun all these years ago, and perhaps now resuming, didn't matter terribly much. The important thing was that it was real. And everything else was not just false, but in some baffling way non-existent. This alone: her in his arms, her face cool and wet with tears against his palm, her warm body wrapped in its coat, and the pretty scarf about her neck, and the fine-boned limbs that he knew to be contained within all her warm and pretty clothes – only this person beside him, and the clear-headed way he felt with her just now, only this was real.

'Come on, let's have a drink,' he said. And again she laughed – if it was a laugh – and they lifted their cups, with a design of diamonds in various colours, probably intended for a child's birthday party, and drank. Even the cups seemed especially significant now: a symbol of childhood, and therefore of the passing of the years. They too helped to shrink time, shrink the length of a life. Life was after all not so very long, he felt; nor so very far: wherever you wandered you never could get very far from yourself, in the end.

When she got up she had already composed herself, and he knew what would happen. They hugged a long time, standing beside the bench. His mind seemed to go soft and blurry, and he lost all track of time, and in the end he never knew how long they stood there, nor how long they had been at the bench. But when she dropped him back at the station, as he knew now she would do, he discovered that five hours had passed. He felt that he had no idea at all what that meant. Was that a lot of time? Or very little? She kissed him on the lips and thanked him several times for coming, and he thanked her for inviting him. He managed to say: 'I think I never stopped loving you.' The words formed by themselves and pressed their way out of him. He was glad they did.

She said, 'Shh,' and put her fingertips to his lips. Her fingers tasted cool and unbelievably fresh, like dew sipped off a petal at dawn.

She leaned her forehead against his and rocked her head gently, and whispered, 'There is too much to lose now.'

And he agreed with her and felt she was absolutely right.

All through the train journey back to Paris, and then the

230

plane back to England the next day, he was carried along by a curious light-heartedness. For a few days he could think of virtually nothing but her. He seemed to have another mind, another voice in his head, along with his own – hers. He had conversations with this voice, he laughed with it, he made declarations to it, he commented on things he saw, and she responded. One afternoon when he ought to have been working in his study at the house, Saskia came home to find him grinning at the kitchen table: sitting there with a grin on his face, for no reason at all.

She glanced at him with a smile. 'Let's hear the joke.'

For a moment he had no idea what she was talking about. He frowned, and that was when he realised he had been grinning. At which point he smiled again, and laughed. 'Just daydreaming.'

She touched his hand and said, 'It seems like an age since we've seen you smile. It's nice.'

Then gradually Celeste's voice faded. Instead, her face began to loom in his mind. Somehow whatever he saw, he saw her face too. At first it was her happy face, then it wasn't, he began to see the frown she had worn just before weeping on the bench by the ravine, and again at the station when she said goodbye to him, and told him there was too much to lose.

One day he had a frightening thought: what if all these years she had in some way longed for him, and felt that their love had never been completed, but now for her it was complete. He had come down and helped her close the door. But that was her door, not his. Somehow while shutting hers, they had opened his. How else to explain the way he felt? Sometimes for half the day he would feel a physical pain in his midriff, a yearning for her so intense it really did hurt.

He called her twice. The first time she was cheerful and polite, and brief. He guessed she wasn't alone in the room where she'd answered. He let a few days pass and tried again, in the middle of the day, when he hoped to catch her on her own.

Before he could stop it he found himself blurting: 'Celeste, I'm thinking about you all the time. I just don't know what to do. What should I do?'

She was silent on the line. Then she sighed and said, 'It's all my fault. I'm sorry. I should never have asked to see you. We both have our lives, our marriages and kids, whatever, our work. I'm sorry. It was stupid and selfish of me. I was curious, I wanted to see you again, just for me, for my own benefit. I didn't mean to upset you. I'm sorry. Please forgive me. And forget me. Please. Maybe I'll write to you. Maybe not. But we mustn't be in touch, it'll ruin everything.'

Mortimer was astonished to hear these words; they were so melodramatic. Were the two of them really caught up in some kind of romantic drama? Somehow it seemed scarcely credible. Yet the way he felt surely suggested they were. Or could be.

After that phone call, at first he felt curiously relieved. For one thing, it was almost as if she felt as he did, that the price of closing her door on their past was to have opened his own. And he knew now he had no choice but to forget about it; there was no future to hope for. It was good to know where he stood.

He managed to acquire a second column in the paper around this time, and got very busy. He was out to dinner at some new restaurant, or at an old favourite, virtually every day now. He drank ever more heavily. On the Lethe-like tide of drink that he allowed to take over his life and carry him off, Celeste shone as a beacon for a while, then he was simply too far from shore, and she dwindled, and went out.

3

Two years after all that he went to New York. When the taxi from the airport rumbled across the grills of the 59th Street Bridge high above the East River, and Mortimer saw the sabres and cutlasses of the world's mightiest army glinting in the afternoon sun, clustered together on their strip of island like a fortress, his heart had exulted in the high sunshine above the silver water.

The very first afternoon, in the corridor of the magazine offices, people had grinned and welcomed him with fierce handshakes. *Good to have you on board. We're lucky to have you.* Right away the editor herself had had Clive and him into her office, a large room with a set of golf clubs in one corner and two banks of windows giving over the city gloriously far below.

'Well, welcome,' she said. 'We're all *very* excited about this.' Then: 'Let's think up some ideas. It's good to have three or four on the go. Don't you think?'

And the two of them, the two old English hacks, had almost fallen off their chairs to agree with her.

In the corridor Mortimer had asked Clive: 'What's going on?'

'They don't forget a Pulitzer here. You're a coup.'

And Mortimer had burst out laughing.

But the stories hadn't come his way. And meanwhile he'd had a couple of scares.

His apartment wasn't much to write home about: a dingy one-bed at the Chelsea Hotel, with floorboards that squeaked and undulated as you walked, and black wallpaper that might once have been chic but was coming away at the seams. But it was on the eleventh floor, almost as high as the Chelsea went, and the view over broad 23rd Street was invigorating, contemplation-inducing.

One morning he'd woken to find a black-fringed hole the size of a football in his blankets, and on the floor the smashed remains of both a terracotta ashtray and a tumbler of water. He must have fallen asleep smoking, set the bedclothes alight, and doused them with the water, all without remembering any of it.

Another time something jumped in his chest and for a full minute he couldn't draw breath. A hand squeezed his heart and pulled it from its usual place, making all the sinews go taut. When he came to, his heart was thumping and his head hurt so badly he didn't dare move. It took him an hour to get to his feet, find his coat and make his way to the elevator.

The doctor admitted him for a night, and the cardiologist saw him two days later to discuss the tests.

'While we're in there we'd probably better go ahead

and make it a quadruple,' he said breezily. 'You'll be better off in the long run.'

Was it urgent?

'Take it easy and you could keep going as you are for a good few years. It's more a question of risk. And how active a life you want to lead.'

Active, Mortimer thought: was that the word for his life now?

He decided it had better wait until he got back home to London, though when that would be he didn't know. But he was thankful he had listened when Clive told him to get American health cover.

Just about the only place that felt like home was his local bar after two whiskies.

He gazed now at the rich gold light on its windows, which any minute would be gone, as the sun sank behind 23rd Street. It seemed a kind of miracle that the sun had found its arrow-shot to the bar at all, among all the immense buildings. Then the shade arrived, slowly, then quite briskly, swallowing up the fields of golden light that the windows had become.

He drained his drink and picked up the three-day-old *Times* that was still lying on the bar top, with its one piece of real news, and tucked it under his arm. Bone cancer, it said. He wondered how sudden it had been, he thought that was one that could be swift. He reeled slightly on his feet, though that was neither from the drink nor his own health issues, but from a disconcerting sense of shock. She was gone off the face of the earth. It was the pouring-on of hyssop, the face of the earth seared clean. Soon he too would be gone. Soon enough all people would be gone. Really, he didn't know what to make of it at all. Except that somehow – however missed and bungled it had been – he felt that what had transpired between him and Celeste had been some kind of victory. It made no sense, but it was as if in the face of the love they'd had – even with the two of them messing it up, or with him doing so, him failing to go to her when she had pleaded with him to do so – nevertheless it still somehow made death seem less important. Or maybe more so. Because it was mostly defeat too. He had failed to do the important thing.

Outside, night was falling and the sky had receded from the tops of the tall buildings. If he'd only known any of Celeste's family well enough he'd have written to them, maybe even gone to see them, for whatever end that might have served. But he didn't. Perhaps he'd write to her husband.

Yet something more had to be done.

He went back to his apartment and sat by the window. The metal heater tutted against the wall. Cars hissed by down below, eleven storeys down, the black tarmac gleaming in their lights. Across town a few signs winked on and off. At this height, there was a softness about the city. Through the door into the bedroom he could see the lamp glowing by two stacks of books. He smoked a cigarette, exhaling against the window pane. The stream of smoke ballooned then rose slowly, indecisively up the black glass.

Beyond the window New York sighed and hummed beneath him, and sometimes wailed quietly.

He was in the wrong place: he knew that now.

It was an alarming thought, but perhaps the thing was to go back to the desert, one last time, to the dunes, the place where one might really meet oneself, or God even; where there was nothing but fierce, searing love. Funny that when the stage was empty, that alone was left.

He got up and went to the cupboard. His heart began to race as it used to in the old days. Life was not a gift but a loan: one never knew when it would be recalled. That was a reason for courage, even for recklessness, for anything but caution. Faster and faster his blood ran, he could just about hear it crashing through the veins. Already, as he fetched his bag and threw it on the bed and opened a drawer and commenced packing, already he could feel the desert all around him. This was what he had been waiting for. It was as if just outside the dark walls of his room, there the desert lay, dark orange, with a milky evening sky hovering over it, and a sunset coalescing in the smoky west. He could already see it, already taste it. And the silence of the desert. His heart knew that too. And beside the crackling campfire there sat his one true companion, on the sand, the firelight licking her face.

He wouldn't let himself stop to think. First thing in the morning he would be at the travel agent's with his bag, ready to go.

4

He was sitting by a watering hole in the desert. They had put out from Tamanrasset in a Landcruiser. He could remember all of it – how he'd got there, the look of the young driver, whose name was Abdul – he could remember the way they'd driven through the night and once seen a column of vehicles in the distance, the beams of their headlights like faint brush strokes in the darkness, and Abdul had told him: '*Contrebandiers.*' Mortimer had reflected that there was no cover out here for a smuggler: no gullies or defiles to creep along, no forests, nothing but the vast, unmappable space, and that was all they needed. They hid in the magnitude.

But he could not remember how he came to be here. Surely he had never reached Tamanrasset.

It was midday, and they were sitting with a group of nomads who had come to water their camels at the well. Abdul had known of the well. It took him a while to find it. He had homed in on it, rather than driven straight to it, as if he had some cartography of the desert pre-installed in his brain; or else a magnetic sense for water.

The nomads were sprawled on the ground under a thorn tree with black boughs, while their camels stood nearby, each with a rein tied to a foreleg. One of the men had of all things a canary stashed in his robes. He took it out and showed it to Mortimer. Celeste would have enjoyed that. He could see her wanting to take a shot of the man and his bird. She would have stroked the back of its tiny yellow neck and smiled. '*Jolie, très jolie.*'

The man growled out a phrase in his incomprehensibly deep voice.

Abdul, squatting nearby, translated: 'He says the bird will sing if you give him a cigarette.'

Mortimer went and fetched a couple of packs, which he found in his bag in the Landcruiser, where he knew they'd be. He also pulled out a slice of bread from the food box, thinking the bird might enjoy that. When Mortimer set the things down on the ground the man didn't move for a while.

When he did finally pick them up, Mortimer thought: Such fine fingers the desert nomads have. They are ascetic, sun-cured people.

It was true. The man's fingers were very fine. He tore off a crust and gave it to the bird, which was still sitting on his open palm. The bird thrashed the bread about to break it up.

A web of shadows spread over the men, cast by the dry boughs of the small, black tree they sat under. Mortimer noticed the dull gleam of rifle barrels on the ground among the men's robes. Perhaps they were fighters who had left some other revolt, and were already home again, in their endless dwelling place.

'Where have they all come from?' Mortimer asked, wanting Abdul to relay the question.

Abdul sank to his haunches. After a moment's pause he spoke to the men in Arabic.

Some of them looked at Abdul, then at Mortimer. One man, with short black stubble and shining white teeth, growled an answer.

'He says from the north. I think they are all from different places.'

A man in a white turban muttered something. Then another who had seemed asleep, lying in the dust with his black scarf draped over his face, rolled on to an elbow and spoke in a deep voice that resonated in the pit of his belly.

'Yes,' Abdul confirmed. 'They come from different places. This man has come from Mali, this man from Assamaka. They are Tuareg, from all over here. From everywhere.'

What Mortimer wanted to know was what they were doing here, at this one tiny well in the middle of five thousand miles of emptiness. Where were they going? Why? And who had built the well anyway? When? No one lived anywhere near here. Except, in a sense, these travellers did, in as much as they lived anywhere. The whole desert was their home, they roamed it according to their own buried notions of necessity.

The man with the bird bent close to it and whispered something. The bird shook itself, fluffed up its chest, and began to sing, craning and puffing its neck, releasing a full chorus, an intricate stream of warbling and cheeping with too many notes in it for the human ear to catch.

Celeste would have been delighted. 'But that's wonderful. A canary in the desert. May I?' She would have lifted her camera, which she had around her neck.

And if the man made no response, she would have left it. Mortimer would have noted that he himself would probably have done the opposite, and admired her for her restraint and tact.

'Shall we have lunch here?' Mortimer asked Abdul.

Abdul tutted quietly, and turned to look at the car.

They drove for another hour, then stopped to eat, and

dozed in the shade beneath the car through the early afternoon. Then they drove again, still westwards, towards the sun, and the sand sea where they were headed.

The sun was getting low when they pulled up in another hollow similar to where the well had been. Two of the small black trees grew from the stony ground.

'*C'est bien*,' Abdul said. 'From here it's just an hour to the piste. See that hill over there?'

Mortimer nodded, though he didn't know which hill Abdul meant, nor what piste.

Abdul fetched a machete from the car and began to dig around in the dirt, until he found a length of dry root. He tore twigs and bark off one of the trees, and made a horseshoe of rocks. When his fire was crackling with translucent flames, he used the tip of his machete to open two cans of pasta which he emptied into an aluminium pan.

Mortimer climbed one of the humps of earth nearby to see what view there was.

The sun had just set. There was a milkiness to the evening sky. The diminutive hillocks among which they had camped rolled away to the west, dissolving into an undifferentiated mauve. Perhaps over there the land once again became flat.

He had an urge to take off his shoes and socks. At first the ground seemed a little cool in the evening, then quite warm, then he couldn't tell whether it was warm or cool. It was prickly against his tender soles.

Why had he always loved empty places? A radiant mist of orange spread up the sky, a startling sight, a richer, brighter colour than one would ever have thought possible, a neon glow. Its fringes fanned into a pool of jade, which in turn gave way to an iridescent dark sky, a canopy that came right up over Mortimer's head, over the whole bare planet.

For a moment he could feel Celeste's warm breath against his cheek, in his ear, and smelled the smell of her hair, and of her skin just after she'd undressed, smelling like a garden after a rain shower. It was as if she were here, invisible to his sight but perceptible to every other sense. He had slipped into another world, the world of then. And she had been waiting for him, had found him as soon as he reappeared.

Then there was just the empty desert, a ramp leaning against the red wall of sunset.

Softly he could hear the clink of Abdul cooking, once he caught a crack and hiss of the fire itself. Soon they would spread thick blankets on the ground and bed down under the broad sky. Mortimer could not imagine a better covering for a night than the dark sky, nor a place he would rather sleep.

By the time he walked back down the little hill, his footsteps crunching like toast, the world had grown dark enough to make out the fire's glow under the pan, its sheen on Abdul's dark face. Around their secret camp the boulders and slopes of clay loomed and shone.

www.randomhouse.co.uk/vintage